It was like a

He was thirty-eig... ...first sight. He'd b... ...adult life! He was ...ly not the sort of man to lose his cool on account of a woman, yet he'd reacted like a brash schoolboy in love for the first time. Well, he *was* in love for the first time, and he was glad Emily had knocked him for six.

Now all he had to do was to bowl the maiden over in return—simple! Who was he kidding? There was nothing simple about it...

Margaret O'Neill started scribbling at four and began nursing at twenty. She contracted TB and, when recovered, did her British Tuberculosis Association nursing training before general training at the Royal Portsmouth Hospital. She married, had two children, and with her late husband she owned and managed several nursing homes. Now retired and living in Sussex, she still has many nursing contacts. Her husband would have been delighted to see her books in print.

Recent titles by the same author:

THE PRACTICE WIFE
DOUBLE TROUBLE
A CAUTIOUS LOVING

THE PATIENT MAN

BY
MARGARET O'NEILL

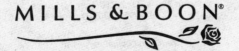

*First published in Great Britain 1998
Harlequin Mills & Boon Limited,
Eton House, 18-24 Paradise Road, Richmond, Surrey TW9 1SR*

© Margaret O'Neill 1998

ISBN 0 263 81284 7

*Set in Times Roman 10½ on 11½ pt.
03-9901-52867-D*

*Printed and bound in Norway
by AIT Trondheim AS, Trondheim*

CHAPTER ONE

HARRY PARADINE, senior consultant of the A and E unit, ran experienced fingers up and down the skinny arms of the old tramp, lying on the examination couch.

'Not a superficial viable vein to stick anything into,' he muttered, half to himself, half to Emily. 'He's hypothermic, dehydrated and shocked. I'll have to do a cut-down and find something deeper to get a line and some fluids in—here, I think.'

Emily, geared through long practice in Casualty to responding quickly to doctors' demands, handed him a scalpel almost before he'd finished speaking.

'Thanks.' He slanted her a quick smile that glinted in his brown eyes. Bending again over the couch, he swabbed clean a patch of papery skin near the crook of the patient's grubby arm and made a tiny incision to expose a vein. Smoothly inserting the cannula that Emily had at the ready, he drew off some blood for sampling, clamped the cannula and left it *in situ*. He handed the full syringe to Emily and she placed it carefully in a receiver to deal with later.

'I'll put in a couple of stitches before we connect up and splint,' he said.

Emily had a skin needle and thread prepared. 'What mix do you want for the drip?' she asked.

He was pulling together the edges of the small wound on either side of the cannula. 'Let's have five per cent dextrose in saline.' He finished his stitching, secured the cannula with a strip of plaster, then strapped and splinted the elbow to keep it straight.

Emily found a bag of dextrose saline solution in the drawer at the bottom of the trolley and hooked it up on the drip-stand. The consultant nodded his thanks and began to connect the tubing to the cannula and adjust the flow of fluid.

Automatically going into the routine for treatment for shock, Emily moved to the other end of the couch and raised the foot by twenty degrees to improve circulation to the vital organs. Then she tucked a heat conserving polarised blanket round the inert form.

The consultant finished adjusting the drip, and smiled at her, revealing large, almost even white teeth, enhanced rather than blemished by a small misalignment between the two top incisors. 'Right, let's have a listen to his chest,' he said.

Emily folded back the top half of the blanket, exposing the old man's grubby torso. His bony ribcage was moving up and down as he drew in shallow, uneven breaths.

Harry ran a stethoscope over the narrow chest and pulled a face. 'Pretty solid. Let's see what his blood pressure's doing.' He wrapped the cuff of the sphygmomanometer round the thin arm. 'Lowish, but better than I expected,' he murmured to Emily. He caught the concerned glint in her eye and grinned reassuringly. 'He's a tough old bird,' he said, his voice surprisingly gentle. 'He'll soon be coming round.'

'Oh, you know him!'

'Yep, he's one of our regulars. The police find him collapsed in some doorway and bring him in two or three times a year.'

'We had our regulars at City Central, too,' said Emily, smoothing back a wisp of dirty white hair from the man's forehead.

The old man's eyelids flickered and opened. Blank

eyes turned frightened and stared up at Harry, who patted his shoulder and smiled down at him. 'Hello, Ed, it's all right, you're in St Luke's Casualty.'

Recognition dawned in the rheumy old eyes. 'Doc,' he croaked. He switched his tired gaze to Emily and frowned.

'This is Sister Prince,' Harry explained. 'She's just joined us.'

The frown cleared, and almost imperceptibly the old man nodded. He licked dry lips and whispered, 'Gawd, I'm thirsty. Can I 'ave a drink, Doc?'

'You can, Ed. We're keeping you in for a few days, same drill as before. We'll give you some antibiotics for that chest of yours and fill you up with fluids.' He raised questioning eyebrows at Emily. 'What would you recommend, Sister?'

She didn't have to be a mind-reader to interpret. 'Tea,' she suggested, 'warm and sweet.'

'Just the ticket,' mumbled Ed, closing his eyes again.

Emily whisked out of the cubicle.

Harry followed her. 'I'll ring Med. Wing and fix up a bed for the old boy,' he said. 'You rustle up the tea and keep an eye on him till they take him to the ward.' He smiled and touched her arm. 'Thanks for your help in there. Nice not to have to dot the Is and cross the Ts. We might have been working together for years instead of for the first time.' His hand still rested on her arm.

Emily frowned down at it and took a step away from him. He dropped it.

Now why did she do that? he wondered.

She said in a husky but rather cool voice, 'Any experienced A and E nurse would have done the same.'

Harry's warm brown eyes searched her lovely face and read— what? Distaste? Sadness? Vulnerability? She had deceptively calm features. He'd noticed it at her interview, this vulnerability and detachment. It made him want to—

He cut off his thoughts and said easily, 'Well, it was nice working with you. Pleased to have you aboard.'

She felt churlish and coloured a little beneath his gaze, but said evenly, 'Thank you, Mr Paradine, I'm sure I'm going to enjoy being here.' She gestured towards the waiting area, at ten in the morning already half-full. 'I'd better give Ed his tea and then make myself useful.'

The consultant pulled a face. 'Looks as if we're going to be busy but, then, what's new about that?' About to turn away and make for his office, he added, 'And it's "Harry" to the staff. We're all on first-name terms here—more friendly. And I'm "Doctor" to most of the patients. The subtleties of being a consultant and being called "Mister" doesn't register with people in distress. They're more reassured by being treated by a doctor or a nurse.

'Just one of our little foibles here at St Luke's,' he said, grinning and showing his nice white teeth again, before he strode off toward his office.

Emily watched until his broad shoulders and handsome head were out of sight, then made off to fetch the tea. His words popped in and out of her mind at intervals during the rest of the day, and it was illustrated that, for all his easy manner, there was absolutely no doubt about who was boss of A and E. The iron fist in the velvet glove, she thought.

Casualty was busy all day and by the time Emily drove out of the hospital gates at five o'clock she'd lost count of the number of patients she'd seen and assisted with: broken arms and legs to be X-rayed and immobilised; innumerable cuts and abrasions to be cleaned and stitched; a couple of coronaries with all their acute needs to be dealt with before they were whisked up to the IC unit.

There had been the occasional lull, but for the most part everyone had worked flat out. Her colleagues seemed a nice bunch: Nurse Manager Jane Porter, whom she'd met at her interview; Jonathan Jones, junior casualty officer, young and rather brash but willing; Nurse Beth Campbell, cheerful and ebullient, and others whose names and faces were as yet a blur.

'So, how do we compare with A and E in your internationally famous London teaching hospital?' Jane had asked with a sly grin, over a belated lunch-break.

'Favourably,' Emily had replied with a laugh, then had added rather more seriously, 'So far as I can see, St Luke's is smaller but just as busy, and the staff are stretched to the limit most of the time—'

'That's par for the course in any casualty department these days,' Jane had interrupted sharply, no longer grinning. 'We had to stretch the budget to take you on, though I've needed an experienced deputy for years. I don't know what you expected, but—'

Emily had broken in quickly, 'Oh, I'm not criticising, far from it. I was going to say that I admire the way that you run the department. In spite of being short-staffed, morale is terrifically high and, I can tell you, it wasn't always that at City Central.'

Jane's fair, plump face had flushed pink, and the engaging smile had slid back in place. 'Glad you think so, but I can't take all the credit. Harry is a super boss—we work as a team. He's an absolute tower of strength yet never throws his weight about.'

'Yes, so I've noticed.'

As she slowed to negotiate the last roundabout at the edge of town, Emily had a sudden vivid picture of Harry Paradine, examining Ed the tramp—his head, with its shock of thick chestnut-coloured hair bent low over the couch, his broad shoulders slightly hunched, his craggy, very masculine face taut with concentration and his brown eyes thoughtful as he ran the stethoscope over the narrow, grubby chest.

How kind and gentle he'd been, taking his time to explain to the old man what he was going to do. And it hadn't been a one-off—she'd seen him repeat the same procedure with other patients several times later in the day.

Jane and the other staff clearly admired and respected him—well, she was prepared to admire him as a doctor just as long as he kept his distance as a man. She recalled his hand lightly resting on her arm and was almost sorry that she had recoiled from it. For an instant it had felt warm and strangely comforting. It had been simply a friendly gesture, but stepping away from him had been automatic. As far as she was concerned, men were bad news, full stop, and better avoided except in the line of duty.

It wasn't rational, but that's the way she felt after the recent pain-filled months—years, if one counted her father's behaviour.

With all her heart she wished that she didn't feel so bitter, and could enjoy men's company as she once had. She sighed heavily and tried to squash her unhappy thoughts, but once started they were hard to stop. They had been triggered off by the new job, meeting new people, Harry Paradine's friendly almost avuncular manner— No, not avuncular, that was too stuffy. He could only be in his late thirties. Reassuring, dependable, that was it.

He was the sort of man one might trust. She snorted with derision—what the hell was she thinking of? She'd had ample proof that no man was to be trusted, not even the Harry Paradines of this world!

She made a final effort to dislodge the doctor's image and succeeded in turning her thoughts to what she and Tim might have for supper.

Harry left the hospital a little after Emily. Like her, he was deep in thought, mulling over the day's events. It was a familiar exercise—reviewing the cases he'd seen, evaluating the way his staff had dealt with the various emergencies, considering if there were any improvements that might be made to make better use of every pair of hands.

Every pair of hands!

Emily Prince had lovely hands—small, neat, competent, beautifully manicured, with shining, naturally polished nails. In fact, everything about her was neat, trim, competent—from her chin-length bob of ebony hair, framing an oval face, to her slender ankles and sensible low-heeled pumps and her firm but gentle handling of patients.

She exuded quiet confidence as she went about her chores. He had watched her quell a couple of noisy youths, reassure the near hysterical parents of a small baby with breathing problems and calm the voluble relatives of a heavily pregnant, beautiful young Indian woman who'd had a fall.

Nothing seemed to faze her. In hours, seemingly without effort, she had slipped into the role as Jane's second in command, and that without raising any resentment from the other staff. Quite an achievement. On today's showing, she was going to be to a valuable asset to the team.

She was on his team—he would see her almost daily! His heart turned over as it had when he'd first clapped eyes on her at her interview a week before. Instantly he had known that she was special, unique. The hairs on the back of his neck and arms had stood up. He had prickled from top to toe.

It was like a miracle. He was thirty-eight and had fallen in love at first sight. This was it, the real thing. Emily Prince was the woman he had been waiting for all his adult life!

He'd tried to talk himself out of it. Love doesn't happen like this, not at my age, wham, bam, out of the blue. But it had and deep in his inner self he couldn't—didn't even want to—deny it.

He had willed himself to be impersonal as the interview had continued, and had given her quite a grilling, asking all the usual questions pertaining to training and her day-to-day approach to her work. So had Manager Jane Porter and the nursing personnel officer, Miriam Armstrong, who were also on the interviewing panel.

Emily had answered intelligently, sometimes humourously, her mouth curving into a wide smile that had reached her sapphire-blue eyes and dimpled her cheeks.

Yet, in spite of her calm and humour, Harry had sensed a sadness, a vulnerability, about her. He would dearly like to know what the hell was bugging her.

The answer to his unspoken question had come a few minutes later when Miriam had asked her why she was leaving a distinguished London teaching hospital to work in a provincial one.

A fleeting expression of pain had flitted across her lovely face. For a moment she had been lost for words. Then quietly she had explained. Her mother had been killed in an accident some months before, and she had returned to care for her young brother who'd been injured in the same accident. If she had continued to work in London she would have had to uproot him at a crucial time in his schooling and take him away from his friends.

'And after all he has been through, I couldn't do that,' she added simply.

Harry wanted to hug her—fiercely, he hoped that her brother appreciated what she had given up for him.

'How old is your brother?' Jane asked.

'Fifteen,' Emily replied. She looked anxious for a moment. 'But having Tim to look after won't in any way interfere with my work,' she assured them. 'He's returned to school and is perfectly able to fend for himself when I'm on duty. And we have an aunt, a great-aunt, living only a few miles away, who would help out if necessary.'

All three of them were satisfied with her explanation and by her reassurances that her work wouldn't be affected. The interview was brought to an end with the assurance that they would be in touch and would let her know their decision shortly.

After Harry had shown her out, Jane said, 'It takes guts to do what she's done—give up her career at City Central in order to look after her brother. Not many women would do that. I liked her. I could work with her. She must be a caring sort of person, just what we need. I vote we offer her the job.'

Miriam agreed. 'I go along with that. She's eminently well qualified but, in spite of that, hasn't asked to be upgraded. She's willing to take the grading and salary on offer. That'll please our masters who hold the purse-strings... What do you think, Harry? Are you in favour?'

Harry, feeling ridiculously pleased that Emily had won his colleagues' praise, was very much in favour. He wanted to shout his support and give the thumbs-up sign, but willed himself to say soberly, 'Let's give it a whirl. I think she'll fit into the team very well.'

Now, recalling the interview as he drove home to the northern outskirts of the town, he wondered what Jane and Miriam would have thought had they known that he was head over heels in love with Emily Prince.

They would think him absolutely crackers probably, though Jane might be pleased. She'd been trying to get him paired off over the three years that they had worked together.

'You're not cut out to end up a grumpy old bachelor,' she'd said on one occasion when he'd politely rejected her latest 'find', whom she had invited to dinner to meet him.

'I don't intend to,' he'd replied, 'but I haven't met the right woman yet. I shall know when I do.'

He drew up in front of the modern, faceless block of flats where he lived.

'And now I have,' he murmured and his heart thumped wildly in his broad chest.

His flat was on the third floor—a set of neat but rather sterile rooms, redeemed by the books lining the walls of the sitting room, a few good prints and the fabulous view over the town.

He poured himself a whiskey—a pure malt, one of his few indulgences when he wasn't driving or on call. He took a sip, swallowed it appreciatively and moved over to the window, where he stood gazing out, seeing not the familiar scene but Emily's lovely face shadowed by sadness.

It wasn't surprising, since she was grieving for her mother to whom she had clearly been very close and was anxious about her brother. So why did he feel that there was something more bothering her—another hurt, an unhealed hurt, a hurt that made her somehow vulnerable? Surely grief over her mother's death and the responsibility of caring for her brother was enough to make her sad.

Sad, yes, but why vulnerable? A vulnerability that made her wary, kept her aloof, on guard. It had been there in her fantastic blue eyes whenever they had met his, both at her interview and today when they were working together, that guarded expression. Or had he imagined it? No! He hadn't noticed that expression when she'd conversed with Jane or Miriam, but it had certainly been there when he had touched her arm and she had looked up at him almost contemptuously.

Remembering that moment, and the way he had smartly dropped his hand, he felt the back of his neck grow warm with embarrassment. He took a large swig of whiskey. What the hell was happening to him? He was a man in his prime, holding down a responsible job, and knew himself to be generally well regarded by his peers.

Off duty he had acquired a reputation for being a self-sufficient, easygoing bachelor, who enjoyed a modest amount of socialising with men and women—his freedom the envy of some of his married colleagues. He was definitely not the sort of man to lose his cool on account of a woman.

He twirled the amber liquid round in his glass and stared down into it. Yet Emily Prince had succeeded in making him do just that, causing him to react like a brash schoolboy in love for the first time. Well, he *was* in love for the first time in the truest sense of the word, and he was not ashamed of it. He was glad that Emily had walked into his life and knocked him for six.

Now all he had to do, to stick to the cricketing metaphor, was to bowl the maiden over in return—simple!

Simple! Who was he kidding? There was nothing simple about it at all. It was crystal clear that the woman

with whom he had chosen to fall in love had some sort
of problem. What was more, he was sure that her problem had to do with men.

If so, he thought wryly, that puts me at a certain dis-
advantage!

By the time Emily reached the WELCOME TO
SHALFORD—PLEASE DRIVE CAREFULLY THROUGH OUR
VILLAGE sign, some twenty minutes out of Chellminster,
she had decided on a mixed grill for supper. A little bit
of everything—sausages, bacon, beans, tomatoes, mushrooms, oven chips—and to hell with the calories and
cholesterol.

It didn't hurt to break out occasionally and Tim, now
that his appetite had returned more or less to the norm
for a fifteen-year-old, would scoff it up. Or would he?
He might, instead, go for a bag of crisps. Emily sighed.
She never knew from one moment to the next what his
mood would be when he walked through the door. He'd
been the same ever since the accident and their mother's
death. Sometimes angry, moody, at others cheerful and
cheeky, like the boy he used to be. He was up and down
like a yo-yo.

'You'll have to be patient with him,' the counsellor
had warned when Tim was discharged from hospital.
'It's only to be expected. He's suffered physical and
emotional trauma and has to come to terms with the fact
that he's been left with a damaged foot and a limp and
he's motherless. Pretty grim at fifteen when you're strug-
gling to impress your peers.'

'Especially as he was an all-round athlete,' Emily had
replied sadly. 'Football, cricket, running, hurdles—you
name it Tim was good at it, but now...'

'Well, he's having physio so his foot might improve

in time. Meanwhile, he's going to need all your support to accept things as they are now.'

'He'll get it,' Emily had promised. 'We'll lick this thing together.'

She had been so confident then, but Tim's mood swings and his refusal to carry on with physio, claiming that it was painful and not working—unusual for him as he was used to the discipline of training for sport—had drained away some of her confidence.

Her hands tightened on the steering-wheel as she slowed to cross the single track over the humpback bridge. If only there was someone she could talk to who knew about teenage boys. They were notoriously difficult at that age. Perhaps she was worrying unnecessarily. Perhaps Tim's switchback moods were due to his age rather than the accident trauma he had suffered.

A man would be useful, someone who knew what it was like to be a teenage youth, bursting with rampant hormones and energy—someone who could empathise with Tim—appreciate what it meant to be fifteen and limited by a disability. If only Mark...

She hissed sharply through clenched teeth. Mark! Empathise with Tim! He had ditched her because of Tim. Even if Tim had been fit he wouldn't have wanted him—he'd made that plain when they'd parted. Furiously she blinked back the tears that pricked her eyelids.

'I'm not into kids,' he'd said. 'They're messy from the day they're born and teenage boys have got to be the worst.'

'You were a teenager once,' she'd replied. 'You must have been messy yourself.'

He'd raised supercilious eyebrows, and a self-satisfied expression had spread across his too-perfect patrician features. 'I was the exception,' he'd said.

They had been engaged for three months, but only then had she finally realised that he was a cold, selfish... 'Bastard,' she muttered under her breath, shivering as she remembered that day.

Still muttering, she circumnavigated the village green and turned off into Old School Lane. 'Why the devil did it take me so long to suss him out, and why—*why*—does it still hurt so much?'

She'd asked herself that endlessly over the last few months and knew the answer—love. Hindsight told her that it been of the rose-tinted variety and mostly on her side. She'd been taken in by his superficial social charm and had translated his faults into virtues, his cold, distant manner into professional detachment and his autocratic manner into authority.

Yet even knowing this, feeling incredibly bruised and bitter, some tattered fragments of love remained, and she mourned its passing.

'Rubbish,' she said loudly. 'What's there to mourn? Thank heaven we split up when we did. Stop feeling sorry for yourself, Emily Prince, and start living the rest of your life. You owe it to yourself and Tim.'

She grinned ruefully. She'd uttered similar words many times over the last few months, but had had difficulty making them stick. Perhaps now, though, with Tim back at school and herself doing the job she loved best, a new life was just around the corner.

Her heart lifted as it always did when she turned into the drive of 1 Lavender Cottages. Home! It had been right to move from the large town-house in Chelminster, with all its memories, to this pretty semi-detached cottage in Shalford. Tim had been all for it. There were people he knew from school, living in the village, and the school bus, as well as regular buses, departed to and from the green. It was easy to get into town.

The lattice-windowed, mellow brick and tiled cottages stood well back from the lane at the top of long front gardens that sloped gently upwards, with narrow, gravelled drives running beside them. Number two was larger than number one as it incorporated what had once been the third cottage in the terrace of farm labourers' dwellings.

It had lain empty ever since Emily and Tim had moved into their cottage, but a week ago a SOLD notice had gone up and three workmen had moved in, wielding hammers and nails and paintbrushes. Over the week their number had doubled to six.

'Having to practically gut the place,' one of the workmen had told Emily when she was working in her garden one afternoon. 'It's a shambles inside—been empty too long.'

They were just departing for the day in a convoy of vans and trailers as Emily arrived. There seemed to be more workmen than ever involved. Whoever had bought the place certainly believed in getting on with the job, and was obviously not short of cash.

After the men had left, Emily stood for a moment and admired the gleaming new paintwork, white and soft leaf green. Whoever was moving in had good taste. It would be lovely if the new occupants turned out to be a family, ideally with boys near Tim's age with whom he might be able to make friends. Or was that just wishful thinking on her part?

Oh, well, it was all in the lap of the gods, she thought wryly as she let herself into her own cottage. Whatever will be, will be.

Tim arrived home some twenty minutes later as Emily was laying the table for dinner by the window, overlooking the garden. She could see at once that he was

in good form as he walked up the drive and she let out
a little sigh of relief. He was limping as usual, but there
was a spring in his step and he wasn't slouching. His
shoulders were straight and square.

He let himself into the tiny hall and she heard him
drop his bag of books at the foot of the stairs.

'Well?' she asked, as he appeared a moment later in
the doorway of the sitting room. No prizes she thought
for knowing what his answer would be.

He beamed at her, and his vivid blue eyes, so like
hers, sparkled. 'We won,' he said. 'Four-two.'

'Brilliant.' It made her happy to see him smiling and
relaxed. Dared she hope that he might remember that
she had started her new job today and ask how she'd
got on, or was that too much to ask?

Tim came further into the room and planted a paper
bag on the table. He said awkwardly, 'This is for you,
Em... It's only chocolates—you know, because of your
new job. Did it go OK?'

Emily stared at the package and then up at him, and
blinked back tears. She could have hugged him. Musn't
embarrass him. She smiled. 'Oh, Tim, how lovely.
Thank you so much. And it went fine. I'm working with
a nice bunch of people. We were busy, but Casualty
always is.' She stopped abruptly. Don't go on about it
or you'll bore him to death, a small voice warned her.
'Dinner's ready when you are,' she said brightly.

'Smells good,'

'Mixed grill.'

'Great. I'm starving.'

It's been a lovely evening, Emily thought as she snug-
gled down under her duvet—the warm April day had
turned chilly once the sun had set. Tim had been happy,
almost like his old, pre-accident self. Spurred on by her,

he had talked football over dinner, giving a blow-by-blow account of the inter-schools match that his school had just won. She had made what she'd hoped were intelligent comments and had inwardly vowed that she would learn more about the game.

After dinner he had, without prompting, tackled his homework. At his suggestion, when he'd finished they had settled down to watch an old, action-packed, war-time movie, scoffing all the chocolates between them, with Tim having the lion's share.

If only he could be like this all the time, she thought sleepily as her eyelids drooped, there'd be no need for counsellors...

She slept heavily and dreamed of Harry Paradine. He was dressed in theatre greens, his craggy features hidden behind a face mask, above which his intelligent brown eyes bored into hers. He was sitting cross-legged beneath a palm tree on a silver-sanded shore, with blue water lapping almost to his bare feet. A neon sign, flashing in the tree above his head, read COUNSELLOR. She and Tim were sitting in front of him at the water's edge, leaning forward eagerly—their eyes glued to his, listening.

CHAPTER TWO

Tim's voice jerked her awake. 'It's nearly seven, Em. Your alarm went off ages ago.'

Emily croaked her thanks, leapt out of bed, dragged on her dressing-gown and made for the bathroom. Hell, she couldn't be late on her second morning. How on earth had she managed to oversleep when she had slept better than she had for months? The answer came loud and clear—she'd been relaxed and happy when she'd gone to bed and had slept on because she was so relaxed. Tim had been at his best, she'd enjoyed her first day at St Luke's, working with Jane and Harry...

Harry Paradine! Her cheeks flamed as she remembered her dream. How could she have sat like a...like a...supplicant at his bare feet? She glowed all over with embarrassment. 'Stop it,' she muttered. 'It's only a dream for heaven's sake—*he* doesn't know anything about it.'

She turned the shower to cold and tilted her face up to the cascading icy needles. After a few minutes under the freezing shower she towelled herself dry, pulled on jeans and a loose sweatshirt, ran a comb through her damp hair, grabbed her shoulder-bag and rushed down to the kitchen.

'I've poured you orange juice,' said Tim. 'Don't worry, you'll make it by half past.'

Her heart soared—he was still in a good mood. 'Thanks, love, you're an angel.' She swallowed the orange juice. 'Have you got all you need—lunch money, whatever?'

22

'Sure, we sorted it yesterday. Go on, get moving.'

'OK, I'm off.' She wanted to give him a quick kiss on the cheek, just as their mother would have done, but wasn't sure if it would be acceptable and contented herself with patting him on the arm as she passed him. 'See you this evening.'

Tim nodded. 'See you.'

As she drove to work she prayed that she would have a breathing space before coming into contact with her boss. The gods were with her. A sharp shower had turned the roads into grease traps for unwary drivers at the height of the morning rush hour, and Casualty was crammed with accident victims. Most, fortunately, had suffered minor bumper-to-bumper injuries, but she and Harry, like everyone else, were kept busy, though in different parts of the department.

It was inevitable, of course, that they would meet up eventually and they came face to face mid-morning just as a woman staggered into Reception, holding a blood-soaked pad to her right eye and whimpering with pain.

'Let's get her into a cubicle, stat,' said Harry, taking the woman's arm.

'Number two's free.' Emily took her other arm. 'What's your name, love?' she asked, as they steered her into cubicle two.

'Nancy,' murmured the woman faintly. 'Nancy Gibbon.'

Harry caught her as she was about to collapse and lifted her onto the couch. Emily raised the bedhead and the knee support halfway down the couch until the patient was in a semi-sitting position.

Together they removed her blood-spattered blouse and jeans and draped her in a hospital gown. Then, very gently, Harry eased her hand and soaked pad away from her eye. Blood was oozing from cuts above and below the eye proper, veiling it completely. Minute slivers of glass glinted in some of the cuts. It was impossible to see if the eyeball itself was damaged.

Nancy whispered, 'It hurts—please do something.'

'We're going to give you an injection to help the pain,' said Harry.

Emily picked up a syringe and unlocked the drawer where the ampules of analgesics were kept. 'Codeine, pethidine...?' she asked.

'Codeine, please, and when you've done that some analgesic cream and spray round the borders of the wound. Then we'll clean up, without disturbing the glass fragments and instil amethocaine 0.25% solution direct into the eye.'

'Nancy, I'm going to give you an injection into your left buttock. Will you twist your hips a little so that I can get to it? That's fine. Now you'll just feel a small prick,' Emily warned as she popped the needle into the firm young muscle.

'Soon have you feeling more comfortable, Nancy,' said Harry, smiling down at her. 'It'll take a little while for the painkillers to work. When they have I'll remove the pieces of glass that are embedded in the cuts around your eye. Now, do you feel up to telling us what happened?'

The story came out haltingly. Apparently, she and her boyfriend had had a row and he'd jabbed at her with a broken-off beer bottle, which explained the circular pattern of cuts around the eye.

'Let's hope,' said Harry, as Emily carefully sponged the blood from the girl's lid, brow and cheek-bones with antiseptic gauze swabs, 'that your eye itself isn't injured. Does it feel as if there is any glass in it?'

'Don't think so—but it don't half hurt.'

'That's because of the cuts around it and pressure

from bruising. The drops will begin to work soon and ease the pain. Meanwhile, if you'll try to keep your eye open for me I'll examine it to make sure there's no direct damage.'

Using the ophthalmoscope, he made a careful examination of the pupil and cornea. He straightened and gave a satisfied grunt. 'That seems clear,' he said, 'but we'll get it looked at by an ophthalmic specialist later on. Now, the spray should have had time to work.' Gently he touched her brow and then her cheek. 'Can you feel that?'

'It feels sort of numb.'

'Right, we'll get on with removing the glass and putting in a few stitches where necessary—fortunately most of the cuts are quite shallow.'

The girl looked scared. 'Will I be scarred—you know, for life, like?'

Harry squeezed her shoulder and gave her a reassuring smile. 'I don't think so, Nancy. Your cuts are mainly superficial and only need pulling together with tiny clips or plaster strips. I promise you that the few stitches I have to put in will be very tiny, and when they come out your skin will be nicely knitted together. In a couple of months' time there'll be nothing to show that can't be covered with a little make up. Don't you agree, Sister?'

Emily, who, while they had been waiting for the analgesics to work, had busied herself, taking Nancy's temperature, pulse and blood pressure, glanced up from the chart she was filling in. Harry's eyes met hers over the girl's head and she found herself staring into their velvet brown depths. In a flash she was catapulted back into her dream, gazing into those same eyes above a green mask, beneath a palm tree on a silver beach beside blue water.

She drew in a sharp breath, felt her cheeks redden and then pale. She frowned at him—Harry wondered why—and smiled at Nancy. 'It's quite true, Nancy. As Doctor says, all the evidence that you've had a nasty injury will disappear.' But not, she thought sadly, from your mind. You'll never forget what your boyfriend has done to you.

Gently she pushed the girl's hair back from her forehead and secured it with a clip. 'Now,' she explained, 'Doctor can get cracking and remove the glass. You'll feel some pressure and some discomfort but no pain. Keep your head still and close your eyes. The injection I gave you may make you feel drowsy.'

Harry was painstakingly meticulous. It took nearly half an hour for him to remove all the debris and for Emily to wash out each cut with saline solution before he closed up. She found herself admiring his rock-steady, smoothly gloved fingers, delicately manipulating the fine forceps as he withdrew the minute shards of glass.

His hands were large, like the rest of him, his fingertips rounded, not long and tapering like some surgeons. Yet he used them as if they were so that the forceps became an extension of his fingers, probing the small wounds with infinite finesse.

They didn't speak while they were working, except to reassure the drowsy patient. There was no need—they worked in unison as they had the day before. Eventually every cut had been dealt with and dressings and antibiotic powder applied.

Harry stood back from the couch and shrugged vigorously, untensing his muscles and stretching the blue cotton of his shirt taut across his broad shoulders. His sleeves were rolled up, revealing his strong forearms and a liberal scattering of bronze-tipped hairs.

'All done, Nancy. I'll leave you in Sister's tender

care.' He smiled at Emily, who, taken by surprise, gave a brilliant smile in return, doing extraordinary things to his pulse rate. 'The eye specialist will be down to see you presently, but I want you to stay put for an hour or so, before attempting to go home.'

With a general smile for the patient and Emily, he left the cubicle.

Emily tidied away the used swabs and receptacles and restocked the trolley. Leaving Nancy to doze, she put up the cot sides on the couch and went off to attend a couple more casualties, returning at intervals to check on her patient.

It was after one o'clock before Nancy, having been seen by the ophthalmic registrar, still a bit wobbly, finally departed in a taxi.

'Where are you going?' asked Emily, helping her into the cab.

'Why, home, of course.'

'You mean, back to your boyfriend?'

'That's where I live.'

'But he beat you up, could have blinded you. Haven't you got a friend or someone you could go to?'

'No. Anyway, he didn't mean to hurt me. He was drunk, didn't know what he was doing.'

How often, thought Emily bitterly, overtaken by a wave of anger as she watched the taxi drive off, have I heard that before? Standing on the sweep of tarmac in front of Casualty in the watery April sunshine, she was suddenly overwhelmed by unhappy memories. She closed her eyes for a moment and leaned against the wall, warmed and comforted by the sun on her face and the warm bricks at her back.

'You look pale. Are you all right?'

There was no mistaking the deep voice.

Emily's eyes flew open and clashed with Harry's. 'I'm

fine, thanks.' She strove to make her voice firm and steady. She produced an artificial little laugh which, even to her own ears, sounded false. 'Are you by any chance keeping tabs on me, Mr Paradine?'

'Harry,' he reminded her. He ignored her facetious suggestion. 'Have you lunched yet?'

'No, I'm on my way to the canteen.'

'For a tired salad and a tasteless apple?'

This time she laughed spontaneously. 'Probably,' she said, 'if St Luke's canteen is anything like City Central.'

'You can bet on it. Come and try out The Peacock in Minster Street, only five minutes away. They do pretty good bar meals.'

In line with her determination to keep relationships with her male colleagues purely professional, an automatic refusal sprang to her lips. She suppressed it. Harry wasn't suggesting a romantic tête-à-tête. Like the good boss that he was, he was being kind and looking after his staff. He'd been concerned for her because she looked pale. As long as he didn't probe.

'Thanks, I'd like that,' she said.

Harry had no intention of probing. He'd sensed her uncertainty and, bearing in mind her reaction when he'd touched her arm yesterday, resolved to keep off anything personal and talk shop.

They pushed their way through the throng of lunch-time shoppers and workers and into the oak-beamed cosiness of The Peacock.

Ducking under the beams, Harry led her to a small table in a bay-windowed recess with a 'Reserved' notice on it.

'The landlord reserves it for me until one-thirty each day,' he explained. 'A one-time grateful patient, or rather his small son was the patient—his father rather thinks he owes me.'

'How come?'

'Let me get our drinks first. What will you have?'

'A white wine spritzer please—lots of spritzer and a dash of wine.'

'I'll join you in that.'

Emily watched him shoulder his way through the crowd to the bar, exchanging an occasional word with people already seated at tables—presumably staff from St Luke's, though there was no one she recognised, but, then, outside A and E she'd not yet met anyone. As men went, Emily thought, he really did seem to be pleasant enough, open and friendly, while as a doctor so far she couldn't fault him.

He had that indefinable quality, flair. Even in the short while she had known him it stood out a mile. It marked him out from the many other doctors she had worked with over the years. Most of them had been competent in varying degrees, some had been brilliant in their particular field but none had had this certain quality.

She supposed it might be comparable to actors or musicians. Some had this quality—genius perhaps, charisma—that made them stars, and others did not.

She pulled herself up with a jerk. What was she doing, sitting here eulogising over the man—no, not the man, she assured herself, the doctor? Of course he was special. As Head of Casualty he had to be an all-round expert— a bit of a GP, a physician, a surgeon, an administrator, with the ability to think on his feet. As far as she could see, Harry was all of these. All things to all men, she thought dryly, or too good to be true?

He was coming back. Emily suppressed the unworthy thought and cursed herself for being so cynical, wishing as she so often did that she could shed her intense dislike

and wariness of men. If only she could put the clock
back to before her mother's death, blot out her father's
perfidy and Mark's desertion...if only.

Harry put her drink in front of her and handed her a
menu. She murmured and smiled her thanks. A sliver of
sunshine slanted through the bay window as he bent over
the table and lit up his chestnut hair, tinting it reddish-
brown.

'You were miles away,' he said softly, as he took his
seat opposite.

At least he hadn't said 'a penny for them'. 'I was
thinking about Nancy Gibbon,' she said. Well, indirectly
that was true. The girl's departure had triggered off her
present line of thought. 'She's going to return to the
bloke who attacked her. I've seen it happen before, but
it always surprises me.'

'I know. It's a sobering thought isn't it, the way
women are prepared to go on forgiving or at least accepting the aggressiveness of their partners? And they
come from all social stratas, not just the poor and badly
housed. There doesn't seem to be much one can do about
it except patch up the damage.'

Emily's fingers tightened round the menu. It was almost as if he knew... Rubbish, of course he didn't. She
said abruptly, 'You were going to tell me why the landlord treats you as a favoured customer.'

'After we've ordered.'

They both settled for soup of the day and fresh bread
and home-made pâté, but this time when Harry returned
from the bar Emily insisted that he told her the story.

'About a year ago Bob's three-year-old son, Ryan,
playing in the courtyard at the back of the pub where
they've got a few tables, picked up and swallowed a
bottle top. By the time they got him round to St Luke's,
things looked pretty grim. He was cyanosed, barely

breathing. It had lodged across his trachea. We couldn't get it out. I had to do an emergency tracheostomy and put in an airway.'

'I hate emergency tracheostomies.'

'I think everyone in the business does. There's an awful finality about it, a feeling of where the hell do we go from here if it fails. Thank God, in most cases it works.'

'Obviously it worked for Ryan.'

'Yes. And though I pointed out that any doctor could have done the same Bob insists on the VIP treatment.'

'I'm not surprised. The effect is rather dramatic—the patient's blue, not breathing, then suddenly pinkens up, comes alive. It always seems especially poignant when the patient's a child.'

Harry nodded. 'That's true,' he said softly, his eyes meeting hers across the table, 'but, then, sick children always tug at the heartstrings, don't they? They seem so small and vulnerable.' He grinned suddenly. 'Though they're not all angels by any means. I've come up against some spoilt, precocious little brats who have rather tested my patience.'

Emily tried to ignore the sensation she had of sinking into the dark depths of his eyes. 'Mine too,' she said, wrinkling her nose and turning down the corners of mouth. 'I feel so sorry for their parents when they play up, though they are probably responsible for spoiling them in the first place.'

Harry wanted to touch the corners of the drooping mouth, run his finger round the full lips. 'While some parents neglect and even abuse their kids,' he said calmly. 'Risky old business isn't it—parenting? Or so I believe. I've no direct experience myself,' he added, for some reason wanting to underline his bachelor status.

As he spoke it occurred to him that parenting was

precisely what Emily was doing in caring for her brother. Did she find it onerous, difficult? A teenage boy wasn't the easiest sort of person to deal with single-handed. Recalling how coolly she had dealt with the rowdy youths yesterday, he thought that perhaps she could.

Had he been wrong about her being vulnerable? No, there was something about her—but it wasn't weakness. That was perhaps wishful thinking, his male ego seeking the opportunity to display his superior strength. No, that wasn't his style and he had too much regard for women for that. Except in a purely physical context when brute strength might be demanded, he had no illusions about women being the weaker sex.

But everyone, male and female, was vulnerable at times. Good Lord, he saw enough of it as a doctor to know that to be true. Covertly, under cover of sipping his drink, he studied Emily's lovely face and longed to share whatever it was that shadowed her eyes when she thought herself unobserved.

Emily was thinking of her role in relation to Tim. Was she, in fact, spoiling him, trying to make up for all that had happened to him? Could one spoil a fifteen-year-old who had once been a cheerful, well-rounded personality? He had been so sweet yesterday and again this morning, not in the least like a spoilt teenager. Surely she couldn't be doing everything wrong!

She sighed, without thinking, and could have cursed herself for doing so. The sigh sounded loud in the silence that hung between them.

'That was a sigh from the heart,' said Harry.

For one wild moment Emily considered confiding in him, only to dismiss the idea instantly. No way was she going to get involved with this charismatic man on a personal level, and to invite his advice, his help, was to do just that. She would sort out her problems with Tim on her own, just as she had been doing since her mother's death.

She shrugged. 'I was just thinking how right you are. Parenting must be like walking a tightrope—' She was interrupted by the arrival of their food, providing a natural diversion and saving her further explanation.

Bowls of aromatic soup, warm French bread and dishes of herb pâté were placed before them.

'Mmm, smells good,' she said.

'Their home-made soup always is,' said Harry, well aware of Emily's relief and wondering what she might have revealed had she not been interrupted. 'Get stuck in. You must be hungry—I know I'm always starving after a busy session and suffering from low blood sugar.'

'You're absolutely right,' said Emily, 'and thanks for saving me from the canteen fodder.'

'A pleasure,' he murmured, wondering if she had an inkling of how much it delighted him to be sitting opposite her.

They had just finished eating and had decided to have coffee when Harry's mobile buzzed.

He fished the phone from his pocket. 'Sorry about this.'

Emily smiled. 'Not to worry.'

He switched on and held the instrument to his ear. 'Harry Paradine,' he murmured into the mouthpiece. He listened intently for a moment, then spoke briskly. 'Right, keep him stretchered until there's enough of us to move him. Be there in about five minutes.'

He retracted the aerial and stood up, turning a rueful face to Emily. 'That was Jane. No coffee, I'm afraid. All hands on deck—a suspected spinal injury coming in shortly. A bricklayer who's fallen off some scaffolding, big bloke apparently. We're going to need at least three each side to move him.'

The ambulance containing their patient drew up as they arrived at the trauma department doors. Jane, Jonathan, the junior casualty officer, and Nurse Beth Campbell were waiting to receive him. The paramedics, with help from Harry and the sturdily built Jonathan, manhandled the wheeled stretcher out of the vehicle and along the wide corridor.

Emily took charge of the drip that the paramedics had set up, Jane held the oxygen mask and bag in position and Beth hurried in front, clearing a passage to the trauma treatment room.

As Harry had predicted, it took all of them to move the injured man from the stretcher to the hard trolley, a combination of strength and expertise being needed. It was imperative to keep the man's head and spine in alignment to avoid damage to the spinal cord. The neck collar helped, but another nurse, Sally Lyons, was drafted in to steady his head during the move while Beth controlled his feet and legs.

The patient, Kevin Strange, who was in his early twenties, had regained consciousness in the ambulance so they were able to explain what they were doing and get a measure of dazed co-operation from him. Once he was safely on the boarded trolley, Jane sent Beth and Sally back to general duties, leaving herself and Emily to assist the two doctors.

Harry immediately despatched Jonathan to contact the orthopaedic consultant and request his presence in Casualty. 'And I mean pronto,' Harry said. 'You don't mess around with spinal injuries—you get in the experts. If Julian Knight's not available, get his sidekick. And let the ortho ward sister know that we'll want a bed.'

Suitably impressed by the urgency of the situation, the raw young doctor scuttled off to the phone.

They all worked quickly and efficiently. Emily and

Jane cut away as much of Kevin's clothing as they could, without moving him, enabling Harry to make a superficial examination. Carefully he ran his stethoscope over Kevin's barrel-like chest, listening to his heart and lungs. His respirations were poor, his breathing shallow but, assisted by oxygen, adequate. There was some muscle response in his arms and hands, but nothing from the waist downwards.

'I'm going to put in a nasogastric tube,' Harry explained to a semi-comatose Kevin. 'That's a tube in your nostril, going down into your stomach, to prevent your guts seizing up.'

'You mean getting paralysed,' muttered Kevin breathily, 'like my legs.'

'Yes, more or less,' replied Harry. 'But you've got some bowel sounds at the moment—that's a good sign.' His voice was quiet and reassuring. 'We're also going to put in a urinary catheter to keep your bladder comfortable, and carry on with the drip that the ambulance people set up.'

While he and Jane inserted the nasogastric tube and then the urinary catheter, Emily busied herself, monitoring and charting Kevin's temperature, pulse and respirations and then his blood pressure. With neat precision, born out of long practice, they all worked round each other to attend to the patient's needs. Like a choreographed set piece, thought Emily, feeling curiously detached for a moment as she completed the TPR and BP chart and prepared a fluid balance sheet.

Beth peeped round the door. 'Can one of you come?' she asked. 'There's a rush on. We could do with a bit of help, sorting the wheat from the chaff.'

'I've finished here. I'll go, you stay and help Harry,' said Jane to Emily.

Jonathan appeared moments later. 'Sorry I took so

long. Mr Knight and his sidekick are both in Theatre,'
he reported, 'but one of them will be down in about ten
minutes. And the dragon sister's doing some shuffling
round to give us a spinal bed, but says not to send up
anyone else as she's chock-a-block.'

'Fair enough,' said Harry. 'You go and hold the fort
out there, Jonathan. Emily and I can manage here.'

Forty minutes later Kevin was on his way to the orthopaedic ward.

Julian Knight himself had come down to look at him
and had confirmed that there was possible spinal damage.

'But I do stress *possible*,' he explained to Kevin with
a surgeon's usual caution, 'because until we do X-rays
and a scan we won't know what the damage is.' His
manner was matter-of-fact, rather detached. 'If there is
damage, hopefully, we can limit it so the sooner we get
cracking the better,' he added. 'I'll see you later in the
ward, Mr Strange.' He nodded, turned away from the
table and made for the door.

Well, he's certainly not brimming over with obvious
TLC, thought Emily, but presumably he knows his stuff
and that's what counts.

Harry followed him to the door. 'Thanks for coming
down so promptly, Julian,' he said.

'Not at all, Harry.' The surgeon gave him a tight
smile. 'If you say it's urgent, that's good enough for
me.'

Shortly after the consultant had left, the porters arrived to take Kevin up to the ward.

Harry patted his shoulder. 'Good luck, old chap,' he
said quietly. 'You're in good hands. Our orthopaedic
team, headed by Mr Knight, is the best.'

Kevin's dark eyes were large and scared and moist in
his pale face. He looked pathetic with his head held rig-

idly between blocks. 'If you say so, Doc,' he muttered in a wobbly voice. 'I dunno what I'd do without my legs, and that's the bottom line, innit—whether my legs are paralysed or not?'

'Yes, it is, but we don't know if that's a permanent condition or the immediate result of the accident that will improve with treatment. There's a hell of a lot being done for people with spinal injuries these days. And the fact that you're going to get immediate treatment from one of the top specialists in the business is a plus. Hang in there, Kevin. You'll have to be patient till all the tests are done but, whatever the outcome, don't give up. You're young and fit—go on fighting and hoping.'

'What good am I going to be to Mary? Might as well be dead,' whispered Kevin, and closed his eyes as the porters wheeled him away.

Harry swore under his breath. 'What the hell do you say to someone like that, Emily? Do you raise their hopes, knowing they might be dashed, or put them fully in the picture and be matter-of-fact, like Julian?'

Emily, busy tidying up, paused and met Harry's bleak gaze across the littered dressings trolley. She would have liked to have said something comforting, but couldn't think of anything. She shook her head. 'I don't know, Harry. After years in A and E, I still don't know. I think you have to play it by ear but, for what it's worth, I think you got the right balance with Kevin.'

'Do you, in spite of what he said about being dead?'

'I do. That was just gut reaction. He'll remember what you said about fighting and hoping at some time in the future.'

'You think?'

'Positive.'

He smiled, the wide, gentle smile that lit up his craggy features and warmed his brown eyes. He said softly,

'Thanks for that, Emily. It's good to have your support. By the way…'

His voice trailed off as Jane interrupted from the doorway. 'Sorry, Harry, but will you come and have a word with Kevin's wife? We managed to get hold of her eventually and she's just arrived. She's in the family room. Or shall I send her straight up to Orthopaedics?'

'No, I'll see her, poor woman.' He sighed heavily. 'This has got to be the worst part of the job, breaking this sort of news to relatives.' He pulled a rueful face. 'Hell, ladies, I sometimes think I'm in the wrong profession—why didn't I become an architect or something?'

Because you care about people, thought Emily as he disappeared into the corridor.

She didn't see any more of him that day or the following day as he wasn't on duty.

'He's reading a paper at a conference in Newcastle on trauma and casualty management,' explained Jane, 'and then he's having some time off so we'll have to get by with young Jonathan and Guy Manning over the next week or so.'

A frisson of disappointment shafted through her—he might have told her that he was going to be away. Or had that been what he was about to do when they were interrupted? She gave herself a mental kick. Why should he explain, for heaven's sake? She was only one of his team and a new one at that.

She said with forced enthusiasm, 'I'm looking forward to meeting Guy Manning.'

'Well, you'll do that any moment now—he's back from leave this morning.'

'What's he like?'

'Pleasant, in his forties, happily married, a bit on the

slow side, but reliable enough. Destined to remain a registrar for ever, I guess. He certainly hasn't got Harry's
flair and know-how but, then, not many medics have—
but they work well together and he seems content
enough.'

For Emily, the next ten days alternately dragged and
rushed past, fluctuating with the workload. As always in
Casualty, it was impossible to predict how busy the department was going to be, and at home equally difficult
to predict Tim's varying moods. From the high of her
first day at St Luke's, when he had bought her chocolates, he either descended into morose silence or was
brashly defiant.

She tried desperately not to mind his near rudeness,
aware that, with the end of the football season in sight
and the athletics season looming, he was acutely unhappy. Everything was a reminder of his physical limi-
tations. He was limping more than usual and, from the
drawn expression on his face, was at times in pain, but
he flatly refused to go for physio or see his GP.

Again she flirted with the idea of counselling, but dismissed it, knowing that Tim would never agree. The idea
of counselling recalled her dream of palm trees and silver sand and, of course, Harry Paradine. She squirmed
inwardly but couldn't get him out of her mind. Like all
the casualty staff, she was missing his guiding hand and
large presence in the department and looked forward to
his return.

With support from Jane, herself and the other experienced nurses, Guy Manning and Jonathan Jones were
coping well, but both of them together couldn't equal
Harry's input, which was more than simply practical.

'Thank God,' said Jane one afternoon when she and
Emily were snatching a quick mug of tea after a partic-

ularly hectic session, when Harry's absence had been most marked. 'The boss will be back in a few days. He'll be delighted that you've settled in so well, Emily. He hates changes in his team, but from the word go you impressed him.'

'We aim to please,' Emily murmured with a self-conscious chuckle as a delicious wave of pleasure washed over her.

'And you do,' laughed Jane. 'Long may it last. I just hope that you don't get restless and start hankering after the lights of the big city.'

'No way. St Luke's and Chellminster is definitely where I belong and mean to stay.'

Jane gave her a long, searching look. 'Of course,' she said softly, 'you have your brother to look after. How are things going?'

It was an invitation to confide and Jane was the sort of woman she might confide in, experienced in the ways of teenagers, with twin eighteen-year-old sons away at university. Emily teetered on the brink, but couldn't bring herself to discuss Tim. It would have seemed like betrayal.

'Fine,' she replied quickly. 'Sweating over exams, but, then, all the kids are at this time of the year, aren't they?'

'Tell me about it,' said Jane. 'Thank the Lord my two are over all that for the time being. They've got a breathing space for a couple of years.'

'Talking of breathing spaces, shouldn't we be getting back?' said Emily.

Emily had the next day off because of working the weekend shift.

It was a bright, breezy, end of April day. If only Tim's mood matched it, she thought, as she watched him slouch down the drive, dragging his deformed foot. He hadn't uttered a word since coming downstairs, just gulped down half a can of Coke and rammed a piece of toast into his mouth. He'd simply grunted when she'd asked what time he would be home, picked up his bag and flung out of the front door.

'And goodbye to you too,' muttered Emily, holding back tears of anger, sadness and frustration as she cleared the breakfast table. She blew her nose hard. 'What you need, my girl,' she told herself briskly, 'is plenty of fresh air and hard physical labour to get your endorphins going—it's a day in the garden for you.'

The morning fled past as she hoed and forked and generally tidied up the wide herbaceous border that ran the length of the garden. Gradually her near despair over Tim faded, replaced by tender memories of her mother who had been a keen and knowledgeable gardener. She looked up at the powder-blue sky and fluffy white clouds.

'You're quite right, Mum,' she murmured softly. 'Gardening's the best therapy.'

She broke off for tea and sandwiches, but was back at work by two. She had just got stuck in when there was a flurry of activity next door. A car swept up the drive, closely followed by a heavier vehicle. Cautiously Emily straightened up and peered over the lavender hedge. A removal van had drawn up in front of the cottage behind an already parked car.

Men piled out of the van. The driver's door of the car was opening. With a smothered giggle, feeling like an inquisitive rustic or an old lady behind a lace curtain, Emily ducked back down behind the hedge. There was a rumble of men's voices and what she presumed was the sound of the van doors being opened.

She waited a moment, then bobbed up again in time

to see a man disappearing through the front door of number two.

Emily gaped—there was no mistaking those broad shoulders, that thick shock of polished chestnut hair. She was staring at the back view of Harry Paradine!

CHAPTER THREE

SHOCKED, mesmerised, as all sorts of wild thoughts whizzed through her head, Emily stood and stared up the long slope of the garden toward the adjacent cottage.

Loud and clear, the message came over—*Harry Paradine was going to be her neighbour*. A quiver of something that felt remarkably like pleasure trickled down her spine. She dismissed it immediately. Of course she wasn't pleased to find her charismatic boss her neighbour. Ridiculous! She had wanted a family there for Tim's sake, and Harry was a self-confessed bachelor who, on his own admission, thought of parenting as walking a tightrope—rather as if he were glad that he had avoided it and wanted to continue to do so.

Questions bombarded her thick and fast. Did he know that she lived in Shalford? Would he be pleased or otherwise to find they were neighbours? Ignoring her panicky first gut reaction, did she mind that they would be seeing one another off duty as well as on? Was she scared of his charisma? Loaded questions—don't know the answers, she admitted. How would Tim feel about it? Did it matter? Whatever they felt, they would have to learn to live side by side with the man.

She must play it cool: with luck they might not see much of him. As a bachelor, he'd probably be out a lot escorting the *crème de la crème* of the social set. His craggily lean face and broad-shouldered masculinity would appeal to a lot of women.

On cue, the doctor's broad shoulders reappeared in the doorway of number two, his face visible only sideways on as he held a conversation with someone over his shoulder. He hadn't seen her yet.

Emily stood rooted to the spot. Every instinct told her to duck behind the hedge, but a mixture of pride, good manners and common sense wouldn't let her. She had to meet him some time— might as well be now. He was a new neighbour and she should make him welcome. Feeling as if she were climbing the steps to the guillotine, she walked slowly up the garden towards him along the edge of the herbaceous border.

Perhaps he would turn and go back into the house— he didn't. He finished his over-the-shoulder conversation and stepped out onto the flagged patio that ran the length of the cottage, moving to one side to avoid two removal men who were carrying a large leather settee from the van. He watched them manoeuvre it through the door.

Emily's heart hammered as she neared the top of the garden, and she slowed to a dawdle. She swallowed. She was within a few yards of him and there was only the border and the hedge between them. He still had his back to her, but any minute now...

Harry pivoted. Saw her. Stood stock-still and stared.

Emily stared back wordlessly. He looked larger, yet leaner, like an advertisement for something healthy, and more masculine than ever in a checked shirt tucked into jeans that fitted snugly over neatly tapering hips and muscular thighs.

She *must* stop staring and say something—anything— like, 'Welcome to Shalford'—or 'Lavender Cottages'. Nothing would come. She ran the tip of her tongue round dry lips.

Her pink tongue moistening the curve of her lips, galvanised Harry into action. Her gesture wasn't a sexy come-on, rather a helpless, childlike gesture, emphasising her vulnerability. He strode across the few yards that separated them, thrust a large hand over the spiky hedge and said in a voice, warm with delight, 'Emily, by all that's wonderful, it's incredible. You would appear to be my neighbour.' His face was wreathed in smiles, and his brown eyes danced. He waited for her to shake hands.

Emily found her feet, though still not her tongue, and carefully picked her way across the border between the golden daffodils, purple irises and sweet-scented wallflowers, stirring up a few early bees and leaving footprints in the newly turned earth.

She reached the hedge and placed her small, grubby hand in his. She discovered her voice and explained inconsequentially, 'Sorry it's dirty. I don't like wearing gloves, you see. I like to feel the earth and plants with my fingers.' Then belatedly she added, 'Welcome to number two Lavender Cottages.'

He squeezed her soil-stained hand. 'Thank you.' His smile broadened still further. 'You'll have to initiate me into the mysteries of gardening. I've spent my working life in flats.'

'You can't exactly teach it,' she replied thoughtfully. 'It's more instinctive or inherited. I inherited the love of it and whatever skill I have from my mother, but it can still be jolly hard work at times.'

'Hands-on stuff, you mean... I think I could manage that.' Laughter lines radiated from his twinkling eyes.

He was laughing at her. He hadn't really been interested in gardening, it had just been an opening gambit. He was flirting with her *and* he was still holding her hand.

He'd made a fool of her. She'd let down her guard for a moment, opened up to him and he was laughing at her and at her enthusiasm. Well, she ought to have known better. He was just another man with a cleverer approach than most. Because she had seen him at work as a sensitive and kind doctor, she had assumed...she had assumed too much.

She felt brittle and hurt. Musn't let him see that. With cool irony, she said, 'Thank you, I'll have it back now.' She wiggled her fingers in his firm grasp.

He released her hand immediately. 'Sorry,' he murmured, wondering why that wary look was back in her eyes and why there'd been the hard little voice that she'd tried to disguise. What had he said or done to put her on the defensive in their few minutes' conversation? Hell, she must have been badly hurt to be so vulnerable.

Or was he overreacting—had he imagined her defensiveness?

Meeting his warm brown eyes, concerned now rather than amused, Emily, too, wondered if *she* had misread *him*. In her bones, she knew that he was a kind man as well as a good doctor. It was just her recently acquired suspicious nature that had made her doubt him. Perhaps he hadn't been laughing *at* her but *with* her or even at himself for his lack of gardening expertise. Anyway, for good or ill, they were to be neighbours so she'd better put right any bad impression that she may have made.

She cleared her throat and asked, 'Is there anything I can do to help? Make you tea or coffee or something? Moving house is ghastly.'

Harry experienced a great wave of relief at this friendly gesture. Obviously he'd misunderstood the expression in her eyes. They were certainly not wary now but clear and very blue, like the cobalt blue in a child's paintbox.

'That's kind of you, but I was warned by a friend to keep the men on the job tanked up with tea and coffee and I'm armed with flasks of the same to tide me over till I unearth my kettle. In fact, I'd better get in there right now and start dispensing.'

'My goodness, you are well organised,' said Emily, and then she said impulsively, amazing herself even as she spoke, 'But come over about six for a bite to eat—save you cooking on your first evening—and you can meet my brother, Tim.' Was she overcompensating for doubting him and overdoing the good neighbour bit?

Harry obviously didn't think so. He beamed. 'I'll accept with pleasure if I may bring a bottle—white or red?'

'White, please. It's a chicken casserole, very simple. I'm not the world's greatest cook.'

'I'm not the world's greatest gourmet,' he said, with a deep-throated chuckle.

It wasn't until she was in the kitchen, preparing the casserole, that it occurred to her what a fool she had been to invite a near stranger to supper—a complete stranger to Tim— without mentioning it to Tim first. She had no idea how he would react. It would entirely depend on what sort of mood he was in when he came home.

Her heart sank when she recalled how difficult and uncommunicative he'd been that morning. Her cheeks burned at the thought that he might let himself down in front of Harry. She wanted to rush next door and take back her invitation but, of course, that was impossible. She must just hope and pray that Tim would be in a good mood when he got home or, if he was not, she could at least talk him into being civil to their visitor.

He came in on the half past five local bus, not the school bus. Did that mean that he'd stayed to watch an inter-house match or something? If he had, had his house won? Emily watched him walk up the drive. Please, God, let him be happy, she prayed. He wasn't exactly bubbling over, but neither was he slouching in his defeated manner. He glanced across at the glowing herbaceous border and then at the next-door cottage.

Emily had left the front door open to let in the west-ering sun and had an oblique view of him from the kitchen window as he entered the hall. His profile gave nothing away. Her fingers whitened as they clutched tightly the potato she was peeling. The moment of truth!

There was the familiar thump as he dumped his bulging bag full of books at the foot of the stairs, then he appeared in the kitchen doorway.

'Hi. Am I thirsty—feels like summer out there.' He loped unevenly across to the fridge. 'Have we got any Coke, Em?'

He was talking! Expelling a silent sigh of relief and unclenching her fingers from the tortured potato, she re-plied happily, 'If you didn't guzzle it all last night.' When should she tell him that they were having a visitor to supper?

Tim gave her a cue. Emerging from the fridge with a can of Coke in his hand, he remarked as he popped the top, 'I see someone's moved in next door—there are curtains at the windows. Seen anything of them yet?'

Turning her back on him and under cover of putting the potatoes in the saucepan, Emily drew in a deep breath.

'Yes, when I was gardening. As it happens, I know the man who's moved in. He's the A and E consultant at St Luke's, head of my department, my boss, Harry Paradine. I spoke to him.'

There, that much had been said. She'd admitted to knowing him so, surely, she was halfway to explaining why she'd invited him to dinner.

'Hey, that's weird…like that clip taken from that old film. ''Of all the gin joints in all the world, you have to walk into mine,''' he mimicked in a passable Humphrey Bogart accent. 'Will you mind, having your boss living next door?'

Emily shrugged. 'No point in minding—it's a *fait accompli*. He seems to be a nice enough man, the little I've seen of him. He's been on leave so I've only worked with him for a couple of days. He's certainly a good doctor so I don't see why he shouldn't be a good neighbour.' She vigorously attacked the carrots with the peeler. 'As a matter of fact, to cement future relations I've invited him over to dinner tonight—thought you'd like to meet him.'

There was what seemed to her to be a long silence, then Tim said, 'OK. Suppose I've got to meet the guy some time or other, but don't expect me to stay and chat to him after we've eaten. I've a stack of homework to do—I'm going up now to make a start. Give a shout when it's ready.'

Not, she noticed, when their visitor arrived—perhaps she was expecting too much. At least he hadn't flung out of the house and refused to meet him. 'OK, will do.'

She checked the time—ten to six. She would put the carrots and cauliflower on for a quick steam at the last minute. Meanwhile, she'd prepare a fresh fruit salad. Well, half fresh fruit. A compromise salad, her mother had called it—tinned mandarin oranges with fresh bananas, apples and grapes. They would have it with ice cream—should suit a non-gourmet's palate and Tim always enjoyed it.

Harry, armed with a bottle, arrived just after six. 'It is chilled,' he said, handing her the bottle of dry white wine. 'I've had my fridge going for a couple of hours.'

He'd added a tie, Emily noticed, to the check shirt. A nice touch, she thought, and was glad that she'd changed from her gardening clothes into a brilliant blue, silky, sleeveless jersey top over a darker blue, mid-calf-length cotton skirt. She knew that the blue top did things for

her, complementing the blue of her eyes and contrasting
with her ebony black hair.

It was clear that Harry thought so too. Admiration
gleamed in the depths of his dark brown eyes as they
swept swiftly over her and came back to rest on her face.

His mouth quirked into a smile. 'Quite a transforma-
tion from jobbing gardener or the trim sister in uniform
to the perfect hostess,' he said, wishing—but not daring—to say so much more.

Emily was suddenly very conscious of the way the
ribbed silk moulded itself to her body, clinging to the
generous curves of her breasts and emphasising her slender waist. Her cheeks flushed as blood rushed into them.
What the devil had made her put on something so...so
feminine? She was giving out all the wrong signals,
which was the last thing she meant to do. Inviting him
to supper was to have been a neighbourly gesture, nothing more.

So remember that, she reminded herself.

'I'll put this in the fridge for another few minutes,'
she said, ducking into the kitchen. 'Do go through to the
sitting room. I won't be a moment.'

He was standing at the window, gazing down the garden, when she entered the room, his broad-shouldered
masculine form sharply silhouetted against the evening
sunlight. Emily paused in the doorway, impressed in
spite of herself by the sheer masculinity of the man. He
seemed to radiate strength and authority.

She crossed the room and stood beside him. He turned
his head and smiled down at her, and for a split second
her heart seemed to stand still. He really had a beautiful
smile. All part of his ammunition, she reminded herself
dryly.

He waved a hand at the garden. 'I'm admiring your
border and wondering if mine will ever match it. It's an

absolute mess at the moment—I don't know where to begin.'

'It's a jungle. You'll have to be ruthless and clear it completely—it's been neglected for years. Apparently, an elderly couple lived in your cottage and couldn't cope. If I were you, I'd get a firm in to do the clearing, get rid of the rubbish and turn the earth over. Then you can sit down and make plans. That'll be the fun bit— the rest will be hard graft.'

She deliberately kept her voice detached and matter-of-fact, determined to keep the rest of the evening on an impersonal level and not give him any excuse to mis-construe the blue jersey.

He pulled a comical face, which did wonderful things for its craggy contours. His eyes were full of laughter. 'Lord, you make it sound like going to war.'

'It is in a way. War on weeds and brambles, creating order out of chaos. Nature needs a helping hand or she literally goes wild.'

'Will you advise me about plants and so on when it gets to the planning stage?'

'Any good nursery will give you advice.'

He shrugged. 'They'd probably talk me into buying all sorts of exotic things that I don't want. I want old-fashioned plants and shrubs that I can learn to recognise and won't dig up by mistake. Besides, I like your ap-proach to gardening, Emily. The tender touch. I'd like to learn to emulate that. So, what do you say, will you take me on?' His eyebrows were like raised question marks, his eyes amused but pleading.

Well, why not? He seemed genuinely eager, and the gardener in her itched to do something about the wil-derness he'd inherited, without making it too formal and contrived. It was a gardener's dream.

She smiled up at him. 'All right, it's a deal, but don't

expect miracles. It takes years to create a garden. I had a good start here, but you'll be starting virtually from scratch. You'll need an awful lot of patience before you see results.'

'Patience,' said Harry, his voice suddenly serious, his eyes locking with hers, 'is my stock in trade.'

For a moment Emily couldn't drag her eyes from his warm gaze. It seemed to envelop her, almost as if his arms were around her and holding her tight to his broad chest. Ludicrous! Nonsense!

Casually—she hoped it looked casual to him—she dragged her eyes from his and down to her watch. 'Time I did something to the vegetables if we're to eat soon. Will you open the wine for me, please, Harry?' she said.

'Be a pleasure.' He followed her through to the kitchen.

'You'll find a corkscrew in there.' She pointed to a drawer. He scrabbled about among the odds and ends of kitchen utensils that she kept in that particular drawer, while she attended to the carrots and cauliflower.

'Shall I take it through and pour?' he asked, as the cork came out of the bottle with a satisfying pop.

'Please.'

'Will Tim have any?'

'No, he'll stick with his precious Coke... Which reminds me, I'd better give him a shout.' Her stomach knotted up at the thought.

'I'm looking forward to meeting him.'

Wish I could guarantee that he felt the same, thought Emily as she called up the stairs. For his own sake I hope he puts up a good front. I don't want Harry, of all people, to think badly of him.

Why not Harry of all people? she wondered later as she lay in bed, waiting for sleep to come. Why was Harry's perception of Tim so important? Because he was her boss, a new neighbour with whom they were bound to have a close relationship? That was part of it, of course, but it wasn't only that. It was something to do with the man himself.

A man who, for all her caution where men generally were concerned, she instinctively knew to be a man of integrity. A man sensitive enough to understand an adolescent's switchback moods, aggravated in Tim's case by recent traumatic events. Unlike cold, sophisticated Mark, he would not dismiss Tim as a nuisance. He might shy clear of parenthood, but he would have sympathy for a difficult teenager.

Not that Tim had been difficult this evening. The evening's events were etched vividly on her mind.

He'd shaken hands firmly with Harry when she'd introduced them to each other, not diffidently or awkwardly but as if he'd meant it. She'd been proud of him. He'd even joined in the conversation over dinner in a low-key manner and had become voluble, as she'd known he would, when she'd steered the conversation towards football.

It had been taking a bit of a risk because she'd had no idea how Harry felt about the game, but she'd banked on the fact that, like it or not, most men seemed to have some knowledge of it.

Harry was certainly well informed. To her delight, he and Tim were soon deep in discussion about the merits of various teams. But her heart had thudded into her stomach when Harry asked, 'Do you play for your school, Tim? You look as if you'd be useful in goal.'

Why had he said that? He couldn't have touched on a more sensitive issue. He must have noticed that Tim was limping when he'd entered the room. Surely his intuition should have told him... Told him what? He didn't know that the accident had left Tim with a damaged foot. He might have thought that he'd simply had a sprained ankle. Why hadn't she had the good sense to mention it earlier?

Her mouth went dry as she waited for Tim to respond. Would he be angry, sullen, or, what was more likely, get up and slouch out of the room, leaving her to make explanations and putting back the cause of neighbourliness for the foreseeable future.

He did none of these things, but shrugged and said almost casually, 'I was in an accident and got smashed up. My foot's useless, permanently damaged. Before that I used to play in goal.'

She had not been in the least deceived by his casual manner and neither, she guessed, glimpsing the fleeting expression of compassion in Harry's eyes, had he.

'That's tough,' Harry said. 'I noticed you were dragging your right leg. I knew from Emily that you'd been in an accident, but I didn't know that you'd suffered a permanent injury.' He took a sip of his wine. 'Do you get much pain?' He was as casual as Tim had been, his voice matter-of-fact yet sympathetic. It was a technique that worked well with patients in trauma.

Oh, please, don't come over all doctorish, she thought, hoping Harry would pick up the warning. Tim will go wild. Doctors aren't his favourite people.

There was a moment's silence while she waited for the explosion to come or the flat denial of pain which he had sometimes used to fend off unwelcome questions—only it didn't.

Tim stared down at his plate, then up and straight into Harry's eyes. 'Yes,' he said quietly, 'I do.'

Watching them both, blue eyes meeting brown, Emily had an eerie feeling that the moment was important.

'Does physio help?' asked Harry.

'I've given up on physio—it makes it worse.'

'Hands-on massage might help.'

'Massage! Isn't that the same as physio?'

'No—it's complementary. It's manipulation of the soft tissues of the body. Helps keep them subtle, stimulates circulation, helps relieve pain. Some sports clubs employ qualified massage therapists to look after their members. We have one at my club—he specialises in sports injuries. He does some private work outside the club.'

She stared into the darkness, recalling how Tim had stiffened and a bleak look had settled on his face. She remembered his voice as he'd grated, 'But mine isn't a sports injury so he wouldn't be interested in me.'

'He's a dedicated practitioner. The cause of the injury wouldn't be important—it's the condition of your foot now that would interest him. Anyway, you're a footballer so I should say you'd qualify for his help.'

For an instant Tim's eyes had brightened and his pale cheeks had flushed, but had quickly faded. He'd pushed his chair back and stood up, giving Harry a tight little smile.

'Sorry, I've got to go, I've homework to do. Thanks for the suggestion, but I reckon it's like they told me at the hospital. I've got to learn to live with it.'

Harry had turned to Emily after Tim had limped away upstairs. 'Did they really say that?' he asked.

'Not in so many words. They said he had to come to terms with it.'

'This was in St Luke's.'

'No. In the hospital near where the accident happened.'

Remembering, she shivered. She closed her eyes against the memory of that awful day. Of Tim in

Intensive Care, hooked up to monitors and drips, and of her mother, lying dead in the mortuary.

She took a few deep breaths to calm herself. Harry's kind face, as he'd looked at her across the table, swam back into her consciousness.

He said softly, but very firmly, his brown eyes boring into hers, 'You musn't let Tim give up, Emily. Try and persuade him to see this friend of mine. I'm sure that much can be done for that foot of his.'

Wanting desperately to believe him, she said, 'I'll try, but he seems to have made up his mind that he's stuck with it for ever.'

'Then we must do everything to persuade him otherwise. At least we must try every avenue before we give up.'

The 'we' had been comforting—it was the first time in months that she felt she had some support. A wonderfully warming sensation flooded through her.

At last her eyes began to droop. It was reassuring to know that the cottage next door was no longer empty— doubly reassuring to know that it was occupied not by a stranger but by Harry. She felt *safe*, separated only by the dividing wall from his large, masculine presence. She was infinitely grateful to him for the interest he had shown in Tim—but I must remember, she reminded herself as sleep began to overtake her, that on a personal level I must keep him at arm's length. He's too...too...

Cocooned in the comfort of his protective nearness, she slept deeply and dreamlessly until morning.

On the other side of the dividing wall between the cottages Harry, too, eventually fell asleep. Like Emily, he had lain awake, mulling over all that had happened that day—from the joyful, heart-stopping moment when he'd come face to face with her over the lavender hedge to the moment when they'd parted for the night.

He found it hard to believe in the extraordinary co-incidence that had brought him to Shalford and Lavender Cottages to be her neighbour. It might have taken him months, even though they worked together, to have achieved the friendly rapport that they had established this evening.

That this was largely due to the part that young Tim had innocently played, he readily acknowledged. Just as he acknowledged that, as a doctor, his interest in Tim's condition would have been roused whoever he was— that he was Emily's brother simply enhanced his interest.

Whatever the future might hold for him and Emily, he resolved he would do everything within his power to get Tim's foot right or as near right as possible, however long it took. All his instincts told him that there was a psychological barrier as well as a physical one that was holding the boy back. That his mother's death in the accident might well have something to do with it he didn't doubt.

There was about Tim, as with Emily, an air of vul-nerability. Even on their brief acquaintance it had oc-casionally shadowed his blue eyes as it did hers. Why they were vulnerable, he hoped one day to discover and, if possible, do something about it. Meanwhile, he meant to be there for them, both of them. He surprised himself by how fiercely protective he felt—towards Tim as well as Emily.

That was an aspect, a consequence of loving Emily, that he hadn't expected. He had known since the day she had walked into his life and turned it upside down that she had a dependent brother, though not quite how dependent. Yet the minute he had set eyes on Tim, had watched him limp across the room to shake hands, he had felt curiously drawn to him.

Perhaps because he was struck by his physical likeness to Emily. He had her shining black hair and the same clear blue eyes and high cheek-bones. There the similarities ended. He was tall and would grow taller yet, gangly but with a good pair of shoulders already in the making. That went with him being the all-round athlete that Emily had described when they had sat, drinking coffee, after Tim had left them.

Cradling his coffee-cup, he had watched her expressive face as she had filled him in about the accident that had left Tim not only with a damaged foot but with damaged emotions.

Emily's face had registered both sadness and anger as she'd spoken about her mother's death and Tim's injuries at the hands of a speeding drunken driver. 'Men and their cars and their passion for speed,' she'd said bitterly, her eyes blazing.

He had refrained from stating the obvious—that not all men worshipped their cars or drove when they were drunk. He sighed heavily. Some instinct told him that it was not only drunken drivers at whom her bitterness was aimed—it was against all men. But *why, why*? She'd told him much, but by no means all. What other deep hurt was she hiding? If only he knew, he could help.

So this is what true love at the advanced age of thirty-eight is all about, Harry thought wryly. This desire to share the anguish of one's beloved, to hold her, cherish her, comfort her.

'But I must remember,' he muttered into the darkness as he began at last to drift into sleep, 'that I musn't rush her. She will need handling with kid gloves. As with the garden, the name of the game is patience.'

CHAPTER FOUR

EMILY was due to relieve Jane at two o'clock the following afternoon and arrived ten minutes early to allow for take-over.

She was glad to be on duty. After the surprises of the previous day—her meal with Harry and his positive, reassuring reaction to Tim's problems—she felt in a curious state of suspension, waiting for more to happen—though she was hazy as to what that might be.

Conscious that Harry was next door, half hoping to see him, half dreading that she would, she had kept herself busy and practically spring-cleaned the cottage from top to bottom. In fact, everything had remained quiet, almost ominously quiet, as if number two were still lying empty.

Surely there should be some sounds penetrating the dividing wall. Music, perhaps—he'd told her that he'd already got his centre up and running. The silence was unnerving, disquieting. Where was he? He must have gone out, but wouldn't she have heard his car?

The fact that she had seen neither hide nor hair of him had nagged at her as she had driven into work. Why, she didn't know. He'd unsettled her, got beneath her guard, and she wasn't sure how to respond. That she'd felt safe last night, knowing that he was sleeping next door, had shaken her. It was a contradiction in terms, her terms, not to trust men, and she didn't understand her own reaction.

For months she had been wary of all men, held herself

aloof from them, yet here she was, allowing the where-abouts of her new neighbour to niggle at her.

Just as Tim's near silence that morning before he'd gone off to school niggled at her. He had been mono-syllabic, but thoughtful rather than morose. Was he, too, thinking of last night and Harry's suggestion about mas-sage therapy? He had dismissed it then, but was he hav-ing second thoughts? She longed to ask him, but held back, knowing it wouldn't be wise. This was something Tim would have to decide on his own. All she could do was lend her usual sympathetic ear when he was ready to talk.

A and E was bustling as usual, but not bursting at the seams as it was sometimes. Jane wasn't in the office, and Emily, going in search of her, literally bumped into the solid form of Harry Paradine as he emerged from a curtained cubicle.

'Sorry,' he rumbled, holding her by the shoulders as she rocked on her feet. 'Are you OK?' His eyes gleamed as he searched her face.

She didn't even bother to nod, but breathlessly said exactly what was in her head. 'So this is where you've been all the morning.'

Harry looked surprised then amused. His eyebrows shot up. He had thick, coppery brown eyebrows, she noticed. 'You'll have to explain, you've lost me.'

Emily gulped, clapped a hand over her mouth and stared at him with wide eyes. 'Oh, no,' she murmured, her voice muffled behind her hand. She felt her cheeks go hot—how was she going to explain, without looking a fool? She took a deep breath. 'I—'

She broke off as Beth Campbell popped her head round the curtains of the cubicle next door but one.

'Harry, I think you should come and have a look at this,' she said. She sounded anxious.

'I'm with you,' said Harry. He grinned down at Emily as he dropped his hands, warm through the cotton of her uniform dress, from her shoulders. 'I'll catch up with you later, and you can enlighten me then.'

'Not if I can help it,' Emily breathed as he strode away from her.

A moment's reprieve. She stood with her palms pressed against her hot cheeks as she gathered her wits. Whatever had made her blurt out her thoughts as she had? If he did pin her down—and she had a nasty feeling that he would, however much she tried to avoid him— what was she going to say to him?

"I wondered where you were when I didn't hear you moving about next door or catch a glimpse of you from the windows." Very funny. He would think she was spying on him. And weren't you? asked a cynical little voice in her head. No, she answered firmly. I just hoped to hear someone about because it's nice to know that number two is occupied after all these months. Oh, yeah, said the sarcastic voice.

She was fed up with the voice. 'Yes,' she muttered fiercely.

'My goodness,' said Jane, coming up behind her. 'Talking to yourself. Bad sign old thing.'

Emily whirled. 'Jane, I've been looking for you.'

'I had to make a dash for the loo—been dying to go for hours. Come into the office and I'll bring you up to date.'

Once in the office, Jane went through the notes of patients she had been monitoring who were still receiv- ing or waiting for treatment.

'Nothing dramatic,' she said, 'except for a young lad, thirteen, David Walters—Dave—hit hard in the abdo- men with a football. Harry's a bit bothered about pos- sible internal injuries, though there are bowel sounds and no sign of bleeding. No obvious chest injuries either. But, to be on the safe side, Harry's ordered chest and abdominal X-rays so the lad's waiting for these.'

'Blood samples, cross-matching, just in case?'

'All done. He's on quarter-hourly obs, including bowel sounds. Abdomen's naturally tender so one has to go easy with the stethoscope when doing a listen.' She grinned. 'Sorry, don't need to tell *you* that.'

'Thank you.' Emily bobbed a curtsy. 'Is the boy in a lot of pain?'

'Fair amount, but pretty stoic. Harry's explained that he wants to hold off giving a painkiller until all the tests are done and, preferably, after his parents arrive. Young Dave seems to understand, but I've been popping in and out as much as possible to reassure him.'

'I'll keep up the good work. What else have we got?'

'Ray Miller, seventeen, back of neck carbuncle, waiting for a local to work before being incised and drained. He's in the small treatment room. Been in and out over the last month but hasn't responded to localised dressings though they've kept the area moderately clean. He's on an umbrella of antibiotics which seems to be holding the infection so far.

'Grubby, undernourished, smokes, probably pops something, but no sign of needles. But keep a close eye just in case he decides to have a wander to look for anything. Harry's going to deal with him shortly.'

'Right.' Emily squashed the slight tremor of anger, mixed with pity, that such patients tended to rouse in her. She wasn't here to judge but to treat. Poor chap was probably out of work, bored out of his skull, smoked because—

'Hey, you with me?' said Jane. 'First talking to yourself, now daydreaming. Don't know whether I dare go off and leave you holding the fort.'

Emily held up her hands in mock surrender. 'Sorry—fire away, I'm all ears.'

'Just one other on your list—a Mrs Sheila Connell, fifty, collapsed outside the gates and was helped in by a passerby. Having a heavy menopausal bleed—foot of bed elevated. Blood pressure surprisingly in normal range, pulse rapid and a bit weak, as one would expect. Harry wants her resting, but she'll be able to go home later unless anything unexpected happens. He'll have a word with the husband when he gets here and do a note for her GP. Usual drill, keep pressing fluids by mouth and reassuring.'

'Will do. Now push off and enjoy yourself. Doing anything exciting?'

'Wildly. Washing, ironing, shopping—you know, all that scintillating stuff. But my better half's taking me out to eat tonight so at least I don't have to cook.' She smiled slyly at Emily. 'By the way, I believe you took pity on your new neighbour last night and fed him. That was good of you.'

Emily willed herself not to blush. She managed what she hoped was a light-hearted laugh and grimaced. 'Your spies are everywhere.' There was no mystery, of course. It had to be Harry himself who'd mentioned it, and why not? He and Jane were old friends.

'Had it straight from the horse's mouth. Harry was full of it this morning.' Her eyes twinkled. 'He seems thrilled to bits at finding you his neighbour—how do you feel about having the boss living next door?'

'Surprised,' Emily said carefully. 'You might have warned me that he was moving to Shalford.'

'Didn't know, old thing. I knew he was moving, of course, but he was cagey about where. ''My rustic retreat'' was how he referred to it, ''away from the madding crowd''. Said he was planning to have a house-warming when he'd got settled in.'

'I'd hardly call Shalford a rustic backwater—it's only twelve miles from town.'

Jane chuckled. 'That's rustic, as far as Harry's concerned. Did his training in London and Glasgow, having grown up in Bristol where his parents were in practice. They're both GPs, though they've now retired. He's a real townee with this sudden yen to lead the good life and grow his own veggies or something.'

So the desire to learn about gardening was genuine. 'Oh, well, he's got scope for that. He's got a nice big garden with plenty of potential.' And I'm going to have a hand in it, Emily thought, a wave of pleasure washing over her. She looked at her fob watch. 'Well, I've got work to do. Better get cracking, and you'd better get yourself off before something turns up to stop you.'

They parted outside the office, Jane making for the staffroom, Emily to the cubicles.

She went first to check up on Dave Walters. She introduced herself and did her first set of observations on him—temperature, pulse, respirations, blood pressure and bowel sounds. There was little change from the last obs that Jane had charted, except that his pulse was a little faster and his temperature up a little. He was sweating slightly. Due to pain or something more sinister? Pain, probably.

'How are you feeling, Dave?' she asked when she had finished.

'Sore. My belly aches something awful.'

'Worse than it did?'

'Dunno, it's been going on a bit. I'll be glad when the doctor can give me something for it.'

'I'm going to have a word with him now—won't be a minute.'

Her stomach churned as she went to find Harry—so much for avoiding him and avoiding embarrassment. Patients came first.

He was in the doctors' office, answering the phone. He gestured her in. She waited a moment then said, 'Sorry, can I butt in with just a quickie?'

He nodded and murmured into the mouthpiece, 'Hang on, please. I won't be a jiffy.' He covered the phone with his large hand and smiled at her. Her breathing quickened and her mouth, seemingly of its own volition, smiled back. 'Problem?' he asked softly.

'David Walters, the abdominal in cubicle three. Pulse and temp up a little, pale, sweaty. I think he'll have to have something for the pain. Will you look at him a.s.a.p., I've got to check my other patients.'

'I'm there already,' he replied. Uncovering the phone, he spoke into the receiver. 'Sorry, I've got to go. Emergency. I'll ring you back.'

'It's not exactly an emergency,' muttered Emily, turning to leave the office. 'I just want you to look at the lad before he goes for X-rays.'

Harry placed a large hand on the small of her back and propelled her gently through the door. 'As far as I'm concerned, if you think he needs looking at he needs looking at. I trust your judgement.' He felt her stiffen and immediately dropped his hand—she was still putting out 'don't touch' signals. It was disappointing. He could have sworn she'd been pleased to see him when she'd bumped into him just now.

After last night he'd thought…hoped… Don't kid yourself, he reminded himself wryly. One night of pleasant conversation isn't going to wipe out months, perhaps years, of whatever it is that's bugging her. Don't rush your fences, Paradine.

'Thanks,' she said. 'Unless you need me, I'll go and have a look at Ray Miller and Mrs Connell.'

'You do that. I can manage young Dave and then I'll be through to incise that carbuncle. I may need a hand then.'

Mrs Connell was dozing. Emily surveyed her from just inside the curtains. No point in disturbing her. Rest was the best medicine she could have. Considering she'd had a heavy bleed, her colour was good, just faintly pink, and her breathing was steady. Obviously she'd improved since she'd been admitted.

Ray Miller was sitting on the side of the high couch, naked to the waist. His shaven head and bony shoulders were hunched forward, supported on a plastic-covered pillow on the table beside the bed, exposing the red, angry-looking carbuncle at the top of his spine.

'I ain't moved,' he said, sounding both defensive and aggressive when Emily entered the room, 'but I ain't 'alf getting stiff and my neck's killing me—feels sort of dead, like.'

'That's because the local anaesthetic's working so you won't feel anything when the doctor lances it. He'll be here soon,' Emily explained gently, any anger she'd felt toward the lad evaporating when she saw how thin and emaciated he was. If ever a body could have done with a few good square meals and a good wash, his could, though there was an area extending from his hairline to ribcage which Jane had obviously swabbed with a cleanser to remove the worst of the dirt.

She compared his scrawny torso with Tim's lean but healthy body and could have wept for him. He wasn't much older than Tim. Had he run away from home or been kicked out? Did he live in a squat? Were there squats in the rather genteel town of Chellminster? If there were, she guessed that it had changed since she had lived here, before going off to do her training, or had her middle-class background simply protected her from it as a child?

Her hands were busy laying up a trolley with the instruments, bowls, swabs and dressing pads that would be required to carry out this minor piece of surgery—minor, yet necessary to prevent the infection spreading. Ray's back would need another general wash before Harry applied the antiseptic dye to the immediate area surrounding the carbuncle.

She filled a bowl with warm Savlon and prepared a few swabs. 'I'm just going to give your back a going over, Ray.'

'Wot, another one? Blimey, the other nurse already done it. You'll wash all the skin off.'

Emily grinned. 'I'll try not to do that, love. Just relax, it's nice and warm.'

Harry arrived as she finished her clean-up operation. She was very conscious of his large presence in the small room.

'All done?' he asked.

'Yes, but I'd better go and do young Dave's obs before we start here,' she said.

'No need. He's just gone up for his X-rays. And you were right.' His eyes smiled into hers. 'He needed something for the pain. He was so tensed up he wouldn't have got through the session without it.' He flicked his gaze down to the patient. 'OK, Ray, let's get on with this job. You're going to feel a lot better when it's done, but it'll be a bit sore when the local anaesthetic wears off. We'll give you a few painkillers to get you through the night, but they're for your use, son, not your mates—understood?'

'Yeah.'

It took about fifteen minutes to incise, irrigate and

drain the wound of most of the pus. Harry worked fast, without seeming to do so.

'Leave a drain in and pack it with antibiotic powder and ribbon gauze and cover with a protective dressing,' he instructed Emily. He disposed of his gloves and plastic apron in the bin and gave Ray an encouraging smile. 'It's looking good now. Keep taking the antibiotics and make an appointment on your way out to come in tomorrow to have a clean dressing put on. And remember what I said about those painkillers.'

'OK, Doctor, and—er—thanks.'

Harry nodded. 'Just look after yourself.' He looked at his watch and then at Emily, pulling his wide mouth down at the corners. 'Admin meeting. Should have been there ten minutes ago, but it'll have to wait till I've seen Mrs Connell and her husband. Guy's off but young Jonathan's around somewhere and, with your help, should be able to cope, but buzz me if you need me.'

'Of course.'

Emily found that the rest of the afternoon and evening passed swiftly. There was a steady stream of patients, though they were never under heavy pressure. Just before six o'clock she took herself off to the cafeteria for a late tea and a sandwich.

When she returned to the department it was to find that Harry had dashed in while she'd been gone, but only to check that all was well. She felt a pang of disappointment, quickly swamped by one of relief—at least she didn't have to explain what she'd meant when she'd bumped into him, and surely he would have forgotten all about her outburst when next they met.

'He was off to give a lecture at Porthampton Med School, and Guy's gone off as we're quiet. He's done several long days on the trot, though we can get him at home if needed, ' Beth told her. 'Andrew Carstair's the consultant on call and the SHO is available if needed, but Jonathan's managing fine at present. I think he's revelling in being the medic in charge.'

Emily grinned. 'A great boost for his morale, but we'll keep a close eye on him, Beth, just in case he over-reaches himself.'

Beth winked. 'Understood.'

She needn't have worried. The evening continued to be only moderately busy with minor cases. They didn't have to call in extra help and Jonathan, with experienced nursing assistance to hand, coped beautifully.

A nearly full moon was shining brilliantly when Emily went off duty at ten, paling out the nearby stars and bathing the castellated towers of the famous minster in an unearthly, silvery light.

It was a calm night, warm for the end of April. Leaving the town behind her, she drove with the windows open and breathed in the spring-scented air of the hawthorn hedges lining the narrow country lanes. A fragile, shimmering mist hung over the fields behind the hedges. It was incredibly calm and peaceful.

She heaved a contented sigh. Life was beginning to take on a little colour and meaning since she'd started work at St Luke's a couple of weeks ago—and, she admitted wryly, given a further boost by the presence of Harry Paradine both next door and at work. Of course, it was bound to, she assured herself, he'd been so understanding and helpful about Tim.

Of course, said her inner voice smugly. She ignored it.

There were lights on in her cottage when she turned into the drive, but number two was in darkness except for the porch light. Taking her completely by surprise, a little frisson of disappointment trickled through her and her heart seemed to drop a notch or two. So he was not yet home. So what? It was only half past ten. She wasn't his keeper, for heaven's sake! What the hell did it matter what time he got home?

The twin beams of powerful headlights swung into his drive as she was locking the garage doors. Harry! She experienced a moment of panic. Perhaps he wouldn't see her. In this moonlight? Should she hurry to the front door and disappear into the cottage, pretend she hadn't seen *him*? For goodness' sake, why? What on earth's got into you, woman? Just stay put, wish the man goodnight and then go in.

The car came to a halt on the gravel sweep in front of the garage and Harry slid out. For a large man he moved with a lithe grace. Just as he did about the department, she thought. All his movements were calm and unhurried, as if he'd got all the time in the world. Even when there was a crisis on he exhibited the same calm.

He'd seen her. In a few easy strides he crossed the flagged patio to where the lavender hedge joined the low brick wall topped with trelliswork which separated the two terraces.

'Good evening,' Emily called in a tight voice as he approached. She felt a sense of *déjà vu*—it was a repeat of yesterday when he had crossed to greet her, only this time she remained where she was by her own front door. The moonlight silvered his hair and threw his face dimly into relief. Enough to see that he was smiling.

He drew in a deep breath. 'It's a *lovely* evening,' he said. 'Too good to go in. Come for a walk, Emily, up the lane to the top of the hill.'

Was he joking? No, he was serious.

Taken aback, Emily laughed unsteadily. 'I can't do

that,' she said. 'I've just got home from work. Tim's expecting me.'

'Then pop in and tell him that you're back but you fancy a walk before bed.'

'But he'll think—'

'Tim won't think anything. He'll be glued to the television, watching *Match of the Day*. Come on, Emily, we've both been cooped up for hours—we owe our lungs a little fresh air.' Again he breathed in deeply. 'What's that scent I can smell, sort of velvety and sweet?'

'Wallflowers—they're in my border.'

'I like it. Will you make sure that I have some in my garden when you plan it?'

'When *you* plan it. I'm only going to advise.'

'My ignorance is abysmal. You'll have to guide me through every step of the way.'

She caught her breath. His voice, coming out of the near darkness, was deep, soft, seductive. *No!* She was imagining it, he had a naturally deep voice. And he wasn't exaggerating about his ignorance. Jane had said that he was a complete townee. But even in towns they had gardens.

'Haven't you ever had a garden?' she asked.

'No. When I lived in Bristol, as a kid, we had a courtyard with a few tubs of dusty looking shrubs which attracted all the cats in the neighbourhood. My parents were GPs with a huge, poor practice and were just too busy to think about gardens. Even though they've now retired, they're still living in the same house and doing locum work.'

'So you were born into medicine, as it were?'

'Yep, never wanted to do anything else, except that I chose the hospital circuit and specialised in trauma instead of going into general practice.' He laughed suddenly. 'Hey, come on, that's enough of the third degree. What about our walk?'

Emily laughed too. She had found it easy, talking to him in the milky moonlit darkness, but a walk—she wasn't ready to go walking in the moonlight with any man, not even Harry Paradine—large, reassuring, with oodles of rugged charm.

Charm! Her skin prickled and she shivered. Both Mark and her father could turn on the charm when they chose to...

Common sense told her that their brand of charm was not the same as Harry's. He didn't switch his on and off—it was natural, part of his character, helped make him the good doctor that he was. Just the same, she was still wary of it. She'd have to turn down the walk but be kind about it.

She said gently, 'Sorry, Harry, no walk for me tonight. It really is too late. I want to have something to eat and fall into bed. And surely you ought to do the same? You've been on duty since the crack of dawn. I thought you'd have taken the day off, after moving yesterday.'

'Meant to, except for giving the lecture—that was planned before I'd fixed the date for moving. But the night staff had a problem and Andrew Carstairs wanted a second opinion. Once there...well, you know how it is. You're right, though, the walk was a mad idea. Supper and bed are infinitely more sensible so I'll say goodnight, Emily. Sleep well.'

'And you,' said Emily, putting her key in the lock. 'Perhaps another time. The view's quite something from the top of the hill.'

'I'd like that,' said Harry.

Hope surged through him. She hadn't turned him down flat, she'd left a window open for the future. And she *was* going to help him with the garden and not, he felt sure, just in an advisory capacity. With luck, she would be beside him, grubbing away with her small, capable hands. His heart leapt. He had that to look forward to.

He stood for a few minutes longer, drinking in the scents of the garden and thanking the gods that had landed him here in Shalford, beside his beloved. He had fallen hopelessly, passionately, head-over-heels in love when he had begun to think that love had passed him by. It hadn't, and he was gloriously glad of it.

Now all he had to do was wait for Emily to discover that she returned his love. That she would one day, he had no doubts whatsoever, provided that he didn't put any pressure on her. Well, he had no intention of doing that. She could have all the time in the world.

CHAPTER FIVE

THE last few days of April merged into May, mostly blue and golden but with occasional heavy bursts of rain. Emily was glad of the rain as she didn't relish the thought of watering her wide, long, thirsty herbaceous border. She was working extra hours to cover a nurse who was away, doing a revision course. It was as much as she could do to keep the weeds under control.

She saw little of Harry to speak to, except on the odd occasion when he was getting the car out of the garage and she was doing the same. They would exchange greetings and follow each other into work. Once there, it was very much the luck of the draw whether they worked together, and when they did they were often too busy to talk much.

He seemed to be working all hours, either in the department, attending admin meetings or giving lectures. She would hear him come home late at night and wonder if he had been working or socialising and berate herself for being curious.

She reminded herself that it was none of her business, but she couldn't suppress a niggling disappointment that he seemed to have forgotten about Tim's problem—or at least put it on the back burner. Unless he was waiting for Tim to make the first move. He had, after all, left the ball in Tim's court and it really was for him to take Harry up on his offer.

So why did she feel let down? What more could she reasonably expect Harry to do? After all, he was practically a stranger. By accident he had become her neighbour, but that didn't mean that he wanted to be closely involved with them, in spite of that pleasant first evening.

His offer to help Tim had been because he was a good doctor and a thoroughly generous man—she musn't read any more into it than that. And he even seems to have forgotten the garden, she thought incongruously…not that it was in the same category of importance as Tim's foot, but he had seemed so keen.

That he had not forgotten Tim's problem, or even the garden, she learned a few days later.

She arrived home one afternoon and was surprised to find him sitting at the table on his patio. For once, it appeared, he'd left work before her.

He waved a bottle at her when she got out of the car. 'Good, home at last. Come and have a drink,' he called cheerfully, beaming at her.

As if the last week of silence hadn't happened, she thought, trying to ignore the fillip of pleasure that the smile had triggered. 'But it's only just after five,' she pointed out coolly, 'and I've the supper to get and—'

'Hang the supper—we've got things to celebrate.'

'Celebrate?' Her naturally husky voice rose to a squeak. What on earth did he mean?

'Yes… Come on, Em, don't keep the bubbly waiting.'

Em! Only Tim and her mother called her Em. She had always discouraged it in other people, even as a child, yet somehow it sounded right, coming from Harry. Why? Never mind why. For once do something spontaneous, something you want to do, woman—have *fun*. Unbidden, the thought came into her head that fun had been in short supply with Mark—it was too undignified.

OK, so it would be fun to share a bottle with a neighbour at five o'clock in the afternoon.

Especially if that neighbour happens to be Harry Paradine, whispered a deeper voice. She squashed the whisper.

'Bubbly!' She laughed rather breathlessly. 'Well that's different. What sensible woman turns down champagne after a hard day's work?'

'Exactly,' he said, standing up as she pushed through the hedge where it met the low, fenced wall, separating the two terraces. He pulled out one of the wrought-iron chairs opposite his. 'Well, what do you think?' He waved his hand toward the garden.

She turned her head and opened her eyes wide. 'Oh, great, brilliant. You've had it cleared and rotovated. I am pleased. I thought perhaps you'd forgotten about it.'

Harry filled a glass with pale, gold-tinted liquid and put it into her hand. He touched his glass to hers. Their eyes met over the touching rims. 'Forget your expert advice? Never.' His eyes didn't leave hers as he lifted his glass to his lips and sipped the wine.

He had beautiful eyes, so kind, such a soft, tender brown. Emily's heart beat a little faster and her hand trembled slightly as she raised her glass to her lips. 'Here's to the garden and all that grows in it,' she murmured huskily.

Harry smiled and his eyes crinkled at the corners. 'To the garden.' Tilting his head back and breaking eye contact, he swallowed the rest of the wine in his glass, then poured out another and topped up hers. The expression in his eyes changed, becoming suddenly serious. He said softly, 'But there's something else that I hope may be a cause for celebration, though perhaps I'm jumping the gun a little—it concerns Tim.'

'Tim?'

'I've discussed his condition with Bob Keefe, the massage therapist I mentioned the other night.'

Emily frowned and looked surprised. 'You've discussed Tim?'

'Oh, not by name. I just gave him the broad outlines of his injury and the limp that he's left with. Bob has come across a similar condition with a similar history which successfully responded to massage and controlled exercise. But, to confirm that he can do something, he needs to see Tim, examine him and do some up-to-date X-rays. Do you think you could persuade him to see Bob?'

Emily drew in a deep breath. Her heart pounded with relief. So Harry hadn't forgotten the slender thread of hope that he'd tossed out to Tim that first evening. Of course he hadn't. How had she ever thought that he might? He wouldn't have done anything so cruel.

Right, so Harry had done his bit, just as he'd promised, and with all her heart she was grateful to him. But how would Tim react? He should jump at the chance, but would he?

She replied hesitantly, 'I don't know, Harry, you saw how he was the other night. But if there's a possibility...'

Harry reached out and touched her fingers which had tightened around her glass.

He said quietly, 'Remember that's all it is, Em, a possibility. Can't promise more than that. All I can say is that Bob's hopeful and Tim needs to know that... How's he been lately?'

'Quiet, thoughtful, not so angry. That's why I haven't pushed him. In spite of what he said about living with the situation, I believe what you said the other night made an impression. I thought once or twice that he was going to say something, but he hasn't. Oh, Harry, if he could just be given some hope.'

Harry saw tears glittering in her blue eyes and longed to take her in his arms and tell her that everything was going to be all right.

Fat chance of that, he thought wryly, and said, 'It needs courage to embrace hope, knowing one might get knocked down again. And Tim has already experienced enough knocks. Perhaps he does want to talk, but not to you—you're too close. He may feel the need for a more impartial ear…like mine, for instance.'

He paused to let the suggestion sink in, guessing that it would be hard for her to give up her role as mother figure and advisor to her young brother, even temporarily. She might even resent him for making the suggestion. For the boy's sake, it was a risk he had to take.

For an instant Emily did just that as she came to terms with the idea of someone else advising Tim, influencing him. Then her nursing instincts and love for her brother took over. It was what was best for him that mattered. Harry could be right. Perhaps Tim did need someone else to talk to. She looked into Harry's kind, tender eyes and thought that if anyone could get through to Tim, this man could.

In a firm voice she said, 'You're right. He needs someone else, not just his big sister.' She managed a small smile. 'Do talk to him, Harry, persuade him to see this massage specialist. I'm…' She faltered a little. 'I'm relying on you.'

And you'll never guess how much it cost me to say that, she thought as she stood up and drained her glass. Relying on men wasn't on her agenda.

Harry stood up too. Loving her as he did and having already sussed out that she distrusted men, he had some idea of what it had meant to her to use that word 'rely'.

'I'll do my very best.'

Though that's easier said than done, he thought, returning to the table after she'd disappeared round the hedge. He sipped thoughtfully at the now tepid champagne. First catch your fish… In order to talk to Tim he must somehow engineer a meeting with him that didn't look contrived.

Still pondering on how this might be achieved half an hour later, he took himself into the house to prepare his supper and dispose of the remains of the flat champagne.

The problem resolved itself when fate intervened. *Fate!* Perhaps the same fate that had brought him to the cottage, he thought with a touch of irony when he switched on the television and a flickering and then blank screen stared back at him. He examined plugs, fiddled with switches—nothing.

He swore loudly and fluently, something he did rarely. He liked his soccer, but was not a fanatic and could normally have taken it or left it, but he'd particularly wanted to watch the match tonight. It was his home town, Bristol, versus—

Football and Tim! They went together like fish and chips. Tim would be bound to be watching… *What an opportunity!*

Five minutes later he was knocking on Emily's front door. She opened it almost immediately. She looked flushed, her eyes very bright and her lovely mouth curved into a smile—because she was pleased to see him? Dared he hope? A delicate, lingering perfume enveloped her. She looked—'wholesome' was the word that flashed into Harry's mind.

'Saw you coming,' she said breathily. 'Have you come to talk to Tim? He's watching a match but I can—'

'No, don't disturb him. In fact, I'd like to watch with him, if I may. My set's on the blink.'

Her eyes widened, her eyebrows lifted and she dimpled. 'Really?'

Harry nodded. 'Really,' he confirmed, 'if fortuitously.'

Emily lowered her voice to a whisper, though, with the noises coming from the television behind the closed door of the sitting room, there was no need. 'Would you like me to disappear?'

The last thing he wanted was for her to disappear, but it made sense.

He smiled down at her. 'Might be best. You know, all boys together, enjoy the match and then talk. Do you mind?'

'Of course not.' She touched his bare forearm—faintly tanned, contrasting with the snowy white of his rolled-up shirtsleeve. It still felt warm from the afternoon sunshine, the dusting of curly, coppery hairs soft yet springy. 'Take all the time you need to persuade him, Harry. I'll keep out of the way for as long as it takes.'

She kept out of the way by visiting Great-aunt Meg over at Little Shalford some fifteen miles away.

It was nearly eleven when Emily got home, after playing a high-powered game of Scrabble, at which her erudite aunt beat her hands down.

Apropos of nothing, the strangest idea came to her as she let herself into the cottage—that Harry would approve of her aunt and she of him.

What that had to do with anything, she hadn't a clue.

She stood in the hall, listening to the murmur of voices filtering through the wall, and her stomach churned. Had Harry been successful or not? There was only one way to find out. She took a deep breath, turned the old-fashioned brass handle of the door and let herself into the sitting room.

Two faces turned toward her. Harry's was calm as

always, but he looked pleased, satisfied. Tim's... Tim's usually pale face—he had the same creamy skin that she had—was flushed, his eyes bright.

He jumped up and limped over to her. 'Em.' His voice was crackly with excitement. 'Harry has spoken to the massage therapist he mentioned the other night—remember?'

With a lump in her throat, she nodded.

'Well, he thinks this massage therapy chap, Bob Keefe, can do something for my foot, you know, so that I won't limp any more—'

Harry's deep voice interrupted. 'Not *can*, Tim, *might* be able to, and it'll take time. There'll be no short cuts and you'll have to work hard. It won't be any easier or quicker to show results than the physiotherapy that you gave up on.'

'Oh, I know, you've explained all that.' Tim waved his hand dismissively. 'But, you see, he's *hopeful*. Up to now everyone—psychiatrists, counsellors—kept on about coming to terms with it, as if I'll have to limp around with it all my life like a... ' He scowled. 'Like a cripple. But now, you see, Em, there's hope and I'd like to give it a try.'

Emily dropped her bag to the floor, stood on tiptoe, put her arms around him and hugged him. 'Oh, Tim, that's the best news ever.' She peeped over his shoulder and met Harry's eyes. 'Thank you,' she mouthed.

He smiled, his eyes crinkling at the corners, nodded and mouthed back, 'A pleasure.'

For a fleeting moment Emily felt that there was a fragile, translucent cord between them, drawing them together across the room.

They talked a little longer, agreeing that Harry should get in touch with the therapist and arrange an appointment for Tim as soon as possible.

'Like yesterday, please, Harry,' said Tim with a cheeky grin. Then, suddenly serious and rather awkward, he added, 'I don't know how to thank you, listening to me sounding off...'

'By sticking it out, old son, and proving all those doubting Thomases wrong. And, remember, you've got back-up. Your sister's always been there for you, and from now on I'd like you to think of me being there for you too.'

'Thanks,' murmured Tim. 'And to you too, Em. I've never said, but you've been brilliant since Mum died.'

Emily felt a prickling at the back of her eyes. She produced a laugh. 'Oh, stop buttering me up and get off to bed before you say something you'll regret.'

He grinned back at her. 'You could be right. OK. I'm off. 'Night.'

'This is how he used to be before the accident,' said Emily, smiling tremulously at Harry as they listened to Tim, clumping up the stairs. 'My mother used to say that she was lucky—he wasn't like some young lads, always in trouble. He spent his free time running or jumping or playing football or cricket, and most of his friends were the same. I was terrified when he had to give it up that he might get into drugs.'

Harry crossed the room and stood, looking down at her. He put his hands on her shoulders. He felt her tremble slightly, but she didn't shrink away.

'But he didn't,' he said softly, 'and that was all down to you, Em.'

She shook her head. 'No, it was Tim himself. I was so scared that I tackled him about it, asked him if he'd been tempted. He said no way, his body was enough of a mess without drugs. He's always been good at being tough on himself because of his sport. That's why it's been difficult, coping with him being apathetic. It's so out of character.'

Harry rubbed her shoulders gently with the flat of his palms, using rhythmic circular movements.

'It's this tough streak that's going to get him through these next few months. It simply needed a kick-start,' he said. 'But, even so, there may be times when he'll feel like giving up.'

Emily shook her head again. 'No,' she said firmly, 'not now. You've given him *hope*, Harry, and for that I'm so grateful I could kiss you.'

His hands stopped their rhythmic movement. Surprise sparked in the depths of his eyes. He bent his head. 'Be my guest,' he said.

Was she imagining it or did he sound a trifle out of breath? Even with his head bent, she had to stretch up to reach him. She brushed his lips with hers. 'Thank you,' she murmured.

He gripped her shoulders hard for a moment, then abruptly let them go. 'The thanks are all mine,' he said gruffly. 'Goodnight.' He turned smartly on his heel and marched out of the room.

Before she could move she heard the front door being closed.

Now, what had all that been about? Emily mused as she locked doors, switched off lights and made her way up to bed a few minutes later. It was the nearest she'd ever seen Harry thrown off balance—or was she being fanciful? Surely a little kiss hadn't disturbed a sophisticated man like him?

Not that it mattered. It had been a wonderful evening. *He'd* been wonderful and she was glad that she'd kissed him. Though he'd been startled. She hoped he hadn't minded—hadn't thought her pushy or got the wrong idea.

No, he wouldn't do that, he was far too mature and sensible. She experienced a moment's panic. It was the last thing she wanted to happen. But Harry would take it at face value, as she had meant it, she assured herself, an expression of her gratitude for what he had done for Tim.

Oh really, butted in a sly inner voice. Then what about that moment when you met his eyes over Tim's shoulder...what did that mean?

'Nothing, a figment of my imagination—forget it,' Emily said under her breath.

If you say so.

'I do,' she said loudly, confidently.

The voice subsided.

She crossed to the window and stared out at the indigo sky full of bright stars, undimmed by street lighting. So unlike London, where they were hardly visible. For London, read Mark and loving and loathing and a painful parting. Suddenly, for the first time in months, she found herself thinking about him without pain.

He'd left her scarred and battered, but he didn't matter any more. He and London seemed far away and unimportant. This was where she wanted to be. She heaved a sigh of contentment. She felt at peace with the world.

Harry stood in the garden, breathing in the scent of Emily's wallflowers and other sweet fragrances. He wondered what she had thought of his abrupt departure. Had he given himself away, let her see that her thank-you kiss had shaken him rigid? And if he had, had he frightened her off—threatened her precious defences? He must be extra cautious in the future—make sure she saw him as a trustworthy friend, nothing more.

All in all, though, it had been a satisfying evening. He'd got close to Tim. It was good to see the withdrawn boy transformed into an animated, happy, hopeful youth. He felt a brief flush of anger. Why had all the professionals Tim had seen made coming to terms with his lameness a priority, apparently dismissing the idea of a cure?

OK, so they were right not to hold out false hopes, but couldn't they see that they didn't *have* to be false? Why hadn't they taken into account the fact that they were dealing with an intelligent, athletic lad who was used to self-discipline? And what about Emily, a professional nurse, supportive of her brother? Why hadn't they *talked* to her and to Tim and listened to what they'd had to say?

That was good medicine. If they had then the last few months might have been less traumatic for both Tim and Emily—given them both a goal to work towards. Well, that, hopefully, was what he'd been privileged to do tonight.

He heaved a sigh compounded of many emotions as a square of orange light flooded out above his head. He moved back into the shadows and saw Emily appear, sharply silhouetted against the light.

Hardly daring to breathe, he watched as she leaned out of the window and tilted her head upwards to look at the sky. He looked up too. The stars were particularly brilliant tonight, the moonless sky a deep blue-black. How did that old song go...? 'When you wish upon a star your dreams come true!' Perhaps if he wished...

So this was what love did for one, he thought with a wry, inward grin. Turned a healthy, intelligent man, approaching forty, into a superstitious, sentimental fool? The mind boggled. What would Emily think if she could see him standing beneath her window, making wishes?

He glanced up. Emily had disappeared and bright, flowery curtains reduced the orange light to a soft glow.

He sketched a salute toward the glow and whispered, 'Goodnight, dear heart.' Then he strode across the patio and let himself into his own cottage.

'There, you see, Tim?' Bob Keefe, a trim, neat man, looking very professional in a white coat, pointed to the X-ray in the lighted display box. 'The surgeon's done a marvellous job of fixing these metatarsal bones that were mashed to fragments in the accident. According to his report, the muscles and nerves involved were also in a mess, but the neurosurgeons did a marvellous job on them. And the fractured bones in your ankle have responded to physio and have healed nicely in alignment. Things might be a lot worse.'

Emily and Harry had stood back, leaving room for Tim to get close to the screen. They were in Bob's consulting rooms in a fashionable part of Chellminster and had accompanied Tim at his request.

'For moral support,' he'd said with a self-conscious laugh, 'in case...' He'd shrugged. 'Oh, well, just in case.'

Emily knew that he was thinking just in case nothing could be done after all. He hadn't lost hope, but the first euphoria had faded a little. He'd been as taut as a bowstring in the four days he'd had to wait for a consultation.

Now the waiting was over and the moment of truth had come. Bob was about to examine him and give his verdict.

'I shall be some time,' Bob said, turning to Harry and Emily. 'Why don't you take yourselves off for a while? Tim and I will have a lot to talk about after I've finished examining his foot and leg.'

'I think that sounds hopeful, don't you?' said Emily, unable to hide her optimism as she and Harry strolled down the wide, tree-lined avenue.

'Well, Bob seemed to be pleased with the X-rays,' he replied cautiously, 'and the fact that he feels that there will be something to discuss bodes well. One thing we can be sure about is that he'll be honest with Tim, give him a clear picture of what is possible.'

Beside him, Emily gave a little skip. 'Oh, you.' She punched his arm and laughed. 'Trust you to be all cautious, like a doctor.'

Harry chuckled. 'Well, maybe that's because I am a doctor. But you're right, the signs are hopeful. I think Bob would have suggested we stayed had he had bad news to give Tim.'

They found a teashop tucked away in a little street behind the Minster and sat at a window table and ordered tea and cakes.

Not, thought Emily, that I'll be able to eat a thing.

'This is nice,' said Harry, leaning back against the sturdy curve of the old-fashioned Windsor armchair. 'Very nineteen-thirties, like an old movie.'

Like an old, romantic movie, thought Emily, studying him through lowered lashes over the small, round, polished table. He looked relaxed and rather old-fashioned in a tweedy jacket over a lemon turtle-necked sweater. He would have made a super hero, with his craggy good looks, shock of gleaming chestnut hair and beautiful smile.

He was smiling now. 'Have I got a smut on my nose or something?' he asked.

Emily blushed. 'No, of course not.' In a rush she added, 'I was just thinking that you looked a bit like a...like a character in one of those old wartime movies.' At least she'd avoided saying hero!

Harry gave a deep throated chuckle. 'Because of my elderly Oxfam jacket?'

Oxfam! Surely, as a consultant, he didn't have to buy from Oxfam! But perhaps he had dependants, commitments... What utter nonsense. She clamped down on her vivid imagination. Her blush deepened. How had she got herself into this? Why hadn't she invented some reason for staring at him? How could she extricate herself?

She took a deep breath. 'Well, yes, partly. But I'm not criticising... It suits you.' It did. It made him look even more solid and reliable, more masculine...more sexy? 'I'm sorry, I must sound awfully rude.'

He shook his head, his eyes twinkled madly and, as if he had read her thoughts, he said softly, 'Not at all. I don't *have* to buy second-hand clothes—I can afford the odd new suit occasionally.' He leaned across the table and stroked her creamy, rose-tinted cheek with a forefinger. 'Don't be embarrassed, Em. I'm sorry, I shouldn't have teased you about the jacket.'

'It isn't from Oxfam?'

'It is but—'

Their tea arrived—a large, homely, brown pot for two, milk, sugar, cups and saucers and a plateful of cakes.

Emily poured the tea, her hand mercifully steady. She handed him his cup. 'You were saying, about your jacket...' Her voice, too, was steady. She'd got herself under control.

'In a roundabout way it is from Oxfam. A few years ago the hospital put on an auction in aid of some new, state-of-the-art equipment. Among other things, we brought in stuff from Oxfam at a special price to auction off. It was for a good cause. I took a fancy to the jacket and made a bid. I've grown rather fond of it and wear it perhaps more than I should.'

'Oh, no, go on wearing it—as I said, it suits you.'

His eyes smiled into hers. 'I'm glad you think so.'

For a fleeting moment Emily fancied that the silken cord was back in place, drawing them, oh, so gently together. Then the moment had gone.

She offered him the plate of cakes. 'Don't these look good?' she said.

His eyes were still on her face. He helped himself to an angel cake and bit into it. 'Delicious.'

Emily chose a chocolate éclair and immediately regretted it. She nibbled carefully round the edges but some of the cream squelched out. With the tip of her tongue she retrieved most of the cream and chocolate smeared round her mouth.

Casually, Harry stretched across the table and wiped the remainder away with his napkin. 'There,' he said, 'that's better.'

He laughed and suddenly Emily found herself laughing with him. 'Thank you,' she said. 'I adore chocolate éclairs but, really, one should only eat them in private.'

'Exactly. They're my favourite, too, but I prudently turned my back on temptation.'

'Not to make a fool of yourself, like I did,' said Emily. 'But I'm jolly well going to finish it now I've started.'

'Good for you. Waste not, want not, as my mother would say. I'll keep you company with a doughnut— they can be almost as messy.'

He's so kind, thought Emily, helping me kill time, making small talk till we can go back and find out how Tim has got on. She wouldn't think of what would happen if the therapist couldn't help him. She popped the last piece of éclair into her mouth and glanced at her watch.

Harry swallowed the last jammy crumb of doughnut. 'Yes, time to go, I think.'

Tim was waiting for them when they arrived back at the consulting rooms. His face told Emily all she needed to know.

Her heart soared. 'It's all right, he's going to treat you,' she said joyfully.

'Yep.' He waved some papers at her. 'He's great, Em. I've got a list of exercises to do between treatments and a daily progress chart. Bob's on the phone at the moment, but he wants a word before we go with you and Harry.'

Bob's word was more or less what they'd expected. He seemed to take Harry's involvement for granted. He warned them not to expect too much too soon, but to give Tim encouragement and support and ensure that he did his exercises precisely as prescribed, neither more nor less.

'Don't let him think that by doing more he'll push forward his progress—he won't. They're streamlined to fit in with his twice-a-week massage sessions, which I've arranged after school hours. I will reassess them from time to time.'

'Is there anything else that I...?' Emily glanced at Harry and felt a wave of pleasure surge through her. 'That *we* can do?' she asked.

'Massage his foot and leg with the oil mixture that I've given him before and after his exercises. It's good for the circulation and helps keep the skin supple. Let me know when you need more.' Bob grinned. 'But don't do it before he goes out with his mates. It contains lavender, among other ingredients, and they're likely to make rude comments about him using scent.'

A small price, thought Emily, and hoped Tim thought so too.

'Lavender,' mused Harry as they drove home. 'Very appropriate, considering where we live. I'd no idea it was such a useful plant.'

'I dare say that's why we have an ancient lavender hedge between the cottages,' said Emily. 'It was probably planted purposely for medicinal purposes as well as to scent clothes and sachets. It's good for promoting sleep and many other things.'

She twisted her head to speak to Tim in the back seat. He was engrossed in his charts. 'Will you mind, Tim, being drenched in lavender oil?' she asked tentatively.

He looked up and stared at her in astonishment. 'No way, I'll do anything if it helps get me back in shape.' Colour flooded his cheeks. He said fiercely, 'You'd better believe me, Em, next season I'll be playing for the school, even if it is only as a reserve… Nothing's going to stop me.'

Emily turned to face the front. Tim's fierceness was frightening. She clenched her hands in her lap and closed her eyes. 'Please let it happen,' she prayed.

She felt Harry's large, warm hand close over hers. 'Have faith, it's going to happen,' he murmured. 'He's a gutsy kid.'

CHAPTER SIX

A FEW days after Tim had started his massage treatment an outbreak of gastroenteritis, aggravated by the influx of holidaymakers attending the May fair held on the Egg Field beside Chellminster Minster, brought a flood of patients into A and E. Most of them could have been treated by their GPs had they been at home, but as visitors weren't registered locally they turned up in Casualty.

As always with any bug or infection, it was the old and the young who were most vulnerable and subject to dehydration through vomiting and diarrhoea.

One afternoon Emily found herself working beside Harry, treating a severely dehydrated, shocked, eighteen-month-old baby girl, Poppy Liddell.

They both went into action automatically to treat the toddler for shock.

Emily gently elevated the infant's legs and bottom on a pillow and tucked a blanket round her. Her heart went out to the small bundle looking lost on the large couch. She was a sucker for little ones and wanted to gather up the pathetic little scrap and hug her close.

She compressed her lips and reminded herself not to get maudlin. She had work to do. Poppy's skin looked pinched and felt cold and dry as Emily placed her fingers on the fragile little wrist to take Poppy's pulse and compare it with her temporal pulse. It was rapid, weak, uneven. Her breathing was typically fast and shallow, the little chest rising and falling rapidly. Her cheeks, which should have been as round and rosy as her name, were grey and hollow.

Poppy was a very sick toddler.

'How long has Poppy been like this, Mrs Liddell?' Harry asked the distressed young mother. He was working fast as he talked, setting up a paediatric IV line and starting to drip fluids into the tiny body. He bent over to examine the small chest and abdomen with his large, sensitive hands.

'She started being sick yesterday and had a lot of dirty nappies. She was grizzly and wouldn't take any solids but was still taking tiny sips of milk. I thought she just had a bit of a tummy upset, but this afternoon she suddenly went quiet and didn't want to drink anything. She became more and more drowsy... Oh, Doctor, she is going to be all right, isn't she?'

The young woman's voice was quavery and her eyes, wide with fear, fixed on Harry's face.

How often have I heard that anguished question asked? thought Emily as she charted the little girl's vital signs. It's every doctor's dilemma, trying to be truthful without being frightening. She raised her eyes from her clipboard and glanced at Harry's strong face as he explained what was happening to Poppy.

'Poppy is dehydrated and in shock, my dear, but by getting her to us promptly you have minimised the risk of further dehydration.

'We're starting to replace the lost fluid and salt through this tube, but we don't know how long it'll need to stay in or when Poppy will be able to take sufficient fluids by mouth for it to be discontinued. And there may be other tests that need to be done so we must keep an eye on her for a few days at least. She'll have to be admitted to the children's ward where she'll be under the care of the paediatric specialists.'

The young mother looked apprehensive.

Harry placed a comforting hand on her shoulder. 'It's the best place for her, Mrs Liddell. We have facilities for parents to stay with their children so you can be with her all the time. Now, what about your husband—does he know what's happened?'

Mrs Liddell shook her head, and said a tight voice, 'No, nor cares. We're separated...' Her voice shook. 'We have been since soon after Poppy was born. He couldn't take the responsibility.' She blew her nose on a paper handkerchief. 'There's just Poppy and me, but we manage and I take good care of her. She doesn't want for anything, she doesn't go short.'

Harry's kind eyes were full of compassion and understanding. 'I'm sure she doesn't. Obviously you take superb care of her. This gastroenteritis is nasty, but you did the right thing in bringing her here in good time. Now, I'm going to get one of the experts to take a look at her.' He smiled down at her and then across at Emily.

'Will you please phone Paediatrics, Sister, and ask Dr Scullion or his registrar to come down and have a look at Poppy? I'd like to get her up to the ward as soon as possible.'

Emily read the shorthand in his voice, and nodded. 'I'm on my way, Doctor.' She, too, gave Mrs Liddell's shoulder a squeeze as she passed. 'Dr Scullion's a lovely man and a wizard with children,' she said, whisking out of the cubicle to make the phone call.

Still attached to her drip, little Poppy was taken up to the ward twenty minutes later. To her mother's joy and everyone's relief, she was already showing minuscule signs of improvement. Her colour had slightly improved, her eyelids had fluttered open a couple of times and she'd made little mewling sounds.

Glucose had been added to the drip which, at Dr

Scullion's suggestion, had been speeded up slightly, though within very carefully calculated boundaries which would have to be continually monitored.

All this had been explained to Mrs Liddell who, having got herself together, showed an intelligent interest in all the procedures.

With the toddler and her mother gone, and the flurry of activity over, the cubicle seemed empty.

Emily sighed with obvious relief. 'Poppy is going to be OK, isn't she, Harry?' she appealed. 'The signs are looking good, aren't they?'

'Yep, think so. She seems to be rehydrating fast and children are amazingly tough. After dealing with hundreds of them, it still surprises me how they bounce back.' Harry peeled off his plastic gloves and apron and binned them. He said softly, 'That was a heartfelt sigh, you gave, Em. Does it distress you, working with children?'

Again that diminutive. Why didn't she mind it, coming from him? Why didn't she remind him, as she did everyone else, that she had been christened Emily? Because she not only didn't mind it but for some extraordinary reason she liked it!

She met his eyes. The tenderness she saw there made her catch her breath. 'Well, do you find it difficult, nursing children?' he asked.

She said thoughtfully, 'Not children, once they begin to talk, but babies because they can't tell you what's wrong, and they look so terribly vulnerable. I hated it when I did my stint on the special baby unit. Tiny, tiny bodies smothered in tubes and monitors.

'I always wanted to pick them up and hug them—but, of course, that was just what one couldn't do most of the time. You just had to nurse them at a distance, as it were, cocooned in their incubators... And I felt so desperately sorry for their parents, sitting for hours, unable to do anything except be there.'

She gave him a rather crooked smile and shrugged. 'So, yes, you're right—I find nursing babies difficult, but I promise you I won't fall down on the job.'

Harry raised surprised eyebrows. 'It never occurred to me for one moment that you would. You're much too well trained and professional…and, for what it's worth, I think your feelings do you credit. I don't believe in this non-involvement with patients. I like my staff to be involved, as long as sentiment doesn't cloud their judgement.'

He stretched his muscular arms above his head and rotated his broad shoulders. 'Lord, I'm stiff. It's been a long day. Look, we're both off duty so why don't we go home, sit on the patio, unwind and talk gardening plans over a bottle of wine?'

The suggestion took Emily by surprise. She stared at him. Alarm bells rang. It sounded cosy, as if they were an item, a couple, which emphatically, she told herself, they were not. However much she owed him for what he had done and was prepared to do for Tim, however perceptive and kind he was, she must make it clear that they were only friends. New friends, and that chiefly because they were neighbours as well as colleagues.

No, that wasn't quite true. Fate had thrown them together and his generous help with Tim had forced them into a kind of intimacy. So perhaps it wasn't so surprising that he had spoken as if there was an understanding, a bond, between them. Like it or not, there *was* a bond—and, if she was honest, she *did* like it.

Just as she liked the idea of sitting with him and talking gardens. She had overreacted to his suggestion. After all, she'd promised to guide him through the mysteries of gardening. If she did that, it would be a sort of quid pro quo for his help with Tim. Nonsense, nothing could equal that and no way would he want payment in return for his help.

Oh, hell, why was she so muddled? Why did the images of her father, her ex-fiancé, and the maniac who'd driven the car that had killed her mother flip into her mind? Harry wasn't like any of those men. Why couldn't she take his invitation to discuss something in which they were both interested at face value?

She knew why! Because she was afraid, so terribly afraid of letting this charismatic man get under her defences. That he almost had on several occasions she was well aware, but she mustn't let him get closer...exceed the bounds of friendship. She mustn't give him the slightest grounds for expecting anything more from her.

In a rather cool tone she said, 'I've shopping to do before I go home. I'm not sure how long I'll be.'

'Ah,' said Harry, pulling down the corners of his mouth and looking like a sad harlequin. 'Giving me the brush-off, Emily?'

Had he read her mind? And why Emily and not Em? She didn't want to hurt him. She said quickly, 'No, not at all. I'm just pointing out that I might be late. Look, why don't you come and have supper with me? Say half past seven. I should be back by then. Tim's out, so it'll only be something cold.'

The sad harlequin turned into a happy one as Harry's face split into a wide smile. Her heart leapt. It was like the sun breaking through on a grey day, she thought, and immediately struggled to subdue such a fanciful thought.

'No, I've a better idea. Since you'll be late, let me rustle up supper. After we've eaten we'll stroll around my extensive estate and you can tell me what I must do to magic a garden like yours. We'll sip fine wine as we walk and drink a libation to the god of gardening.' His teasing relaxed her, as he'd intended it should.

Emily giggled. 'I don't know that there is one. There's Ceres, of course, but, strictly, she's associated with corn. The harvest festival hymn always comes to my mind when I'm gardening. It seems to embrace all growing things.'

'Ah… "We plough the fields and scatter…" Very appropriate for my barren plot.'

'It won't be barren for long. We'll fill it up with bushes and plants…'

'And "scatter the good seed on the land."'

'Exactly. Now I must dash, Harry, if I'm to get my shopping done. See you at half seven.'

Suddenly she felt exhilarated, happy, and wanted the evening to begin.

Armed with a bottle of wine, she arrived on his doorstep spot on time.

She held up the bottle with a flourish. 'My turn to contribute the wine. Not exactly "fine", which I suspect means expensive, but dry white, cheap and cheerful.'

Harry grinned and took the bottle from her. 'None the worse for that. I'll pop it in the fridge.' He looked at the label. 'Perfect with grilled trout and mushrooms, and I don't suppose the gods will mind what we "libate" them with.'

He led the way into the sitting room, all tan and russet and muted greens. The walls on either side of the fireplace were lined with books. It suits him, thought Emily, restful, warm, yet solid, like his temperament—a welcoming room.

'By the way…' he motioned her to a squashy armchair '…there *are* gods of gardening—Priapus and Vertumnis, somebody's wife. I did a bit of Sherlock

Holmesing, and unearthed them in my battered copy of the *Childrens' Book of Gods and Legends*.'

His light-hearted mood matched her own. She had squashed her earlier reservations and was determined to enjoy this evening.

'Such diligence. Clever old you. You're one up on me. If you put as much effort into the hard graft of gardening, you'll be competing with my patch next year.'

'You'd better believe it. I'm raring to go.'

'It'll cost a small fortune initially. Plants and bulbs don't come cheap and it takes time to grow them on from seed. You really need a greenhouse to do that, and even a small one, like mine, costs a bomb.'

'Not to worry, cost doesn't come into it.' His eyes danced. 'In spite of the Oxfam jacket, I'm not short of a bob or two. Don't forget, I'm a fancy-free bachelor without commitments. You make a list of what's needed and we'll take it from there. Now, let's have supper.'

They ate at a pine table in the roomy kitchen, which comprised the two kitchens of the original cottages made into one.

Supper was delicious. Trout, mushrooms, glistening baby carrots and new potatoes, followed by generous helpings of early strawberries and cream.

'Thank you. That was out of this world,' said Emily, as she finished her dessert. She dimpled a smile across at Harry. 'You're quite handy in the kitchen, obviously.'

He grinned. 'Practically self-taught. As a lone male, it was either learn to feed myself or eat out all the time, and that didn't appeal. I'm definitely a stay-at-home sort of person. I like the occasional small get-together with friends, a visit to theatre or cinema, but otherwise I'm happy to be at home, especially here at number two Lavender Cottages.'

The urge to add 'living next door to you' sprang to mind, but he suppressed it. Grow up, he told himself, that sort of flirting is strictly for kids.

Instead, he said, 'Shall we do our tour of the garden now, and have coffee when we come back in?'

Emily jumped up from the table. 'What a good idea, before the light goes.'

There was nearly an hour of dusky golden sunlight left as they stepped outside into the balmy evening air. They both breathed in deeply and inhaled all the scents drifting over the lavender hedge.

'Heavenly isn't it?' said Harry.

'Mmm heavenly,' Emily agreed, turning her face to meet the westering sun. She closed her eyes.

Like a beautiful sleek black cat, thought Harry, staring hungrily at her. He was mesmerised by the tilt of her head and the glossy black bob of hair swinging back from her face, framing the high cheek-bones and small determined chin. Her black lashes curled against her creamy skin tinted peach by the sunlight.

He longed to stroke her cheek and run his fingers through the silky fall of hair, but knew that it was still too soon for that sort of intimacy. Instead, he took her hand, casually yet firmly. He felt it quiver, but she didn't pull it away.

'Come on, Em,' he said softly. 'Let's get this show on the road—time for the grand tour.'

Emily opened her eyes and looked at him, a dreamy expression in their sapphire-blue depths. She blinked and brought him properly into focus. He looked very masculine, rock-like, with the sun lighting up every plane of his craggy yet handsome face and throwing his nose and chin into sharp relief. He smelt very masculine too, woodsmoky, tweedy, as if he were wearing the famous Oxfam jacket.

She put into words the picture that flashed into her mind. 'You should be smoking a pipe and gazing out over your historic acres,' she said, amusement trembling in her voice.

He gave a rumble of laughter. 'I'm happy with my humble cottage and my single acre, thank you... As for the pipe, I've too much respect for my lungs.' Her hand was still in his, almost as if she hadn't noticed it was there. She was incredibly relaxed. All the wariness seemed to have disappeared... Had he made a break-through?

Emily chuckled. 'There speaks the cautious doctor. Funny, isn't it, when you think of those old films, with the hero and heroine exchanging cigarettes, puffing away, kissing in a cloud of smoke? It looks so romantic, but it's a wonder they didn't all drop dead on the set— I suppose it was a case of what you didn't know wouldn't hurt you.'

'Or ignorance is bliss. I wonder how many of them *did* die of smoking-related diseases?' Harry mused.

'As a matter of fact, I think quite a lot of them lived to a good age.'

'And quite a lot of them didn't.'

Emily said softly, pressing her fingers against his palm, 'For once don't let us get sidetracked into talking shop, especially sad shop, on a lovely evening like this— we said were going to talk gardening.'

He smiled his lovely smile. He was elated. He was holding her hand and his cool, aloof little Emily hadn't withdrawn it or shrugged him off. 'So we did. Come on, then, let's walk and talk.'

Hand in hand, they ambled down the drive separating the wide strips of lawn and long beds of newly turned earth on either side. In the husky voice that he loved,

Emily did most of the talking. He was content to listen and put in the occasional word.

They would fill the beds with shrubs and old-fashioned perennials, she said. She suggested blue delphiniums and smoky pink lupins, canterbury bells, foxgloves and hollyhocks, with stocks and pinks and pansies in the front of the beds, lining the path. And all against a backdrop of roses and honeysuckle, clinging to the mottled old brick wall running parallel to the drive, down the east side of the garden.

She gestured with her hand. 'And on this side of the drive you must have bushes—buddleia for the butterflies, and rosemary and eucalyptus for the scent—and, of course, spring bulbs scattered around in both beds.'

Harry watched her animated face, lit with enthusiasm, and, if possible, fell even more deeply in love with her. Gone was the distant, detached Emily, who had been hurt and who kept men at arm's length. This was a warm, vital, lovely woman whom he planned to marry.

They reached the end of the drive and stood, looking up the long slope of the garden toward the cottages. 'How rustic and charming it all looks,' said Harry, 'even with my bare garden. The lawns look so green after last night's rain. The firm I had in did a good job of cutting. They look so neat, don't they?'

Emily nodded, but pursed her lips. 'Tidy enough, but they need a lot of attention—aerating, rolling, feeding.'

'But I don't want manicured lawns,' he objected, 'just something that's smooth enough to have a fun game of croquet on or kick a ball around with Tim.'

Typical, thought Emily, that he should think of Tim. She wrinkled up her nose. 'Don't worry, you're in no danger of producing a bowling green. Yours, like ours, is meadow grass, full of buttercups and daisies and ladies' slippers.'

'What on earth are ladies' slippers?'

'Pretty little yellow flowers that only grow about an inch high, and look like—'

'*Ladies' slippers!*' they chanted in unison.

Their eyes met and held as they laughed together. The golden evening sunlight turned Harry's brown eyes to amber. Their laughter died away, the silken cord was back. They stared at each other in sudden silence.

What was happening? Emily could feel her heart beating a rapid tattoo in her heaving chest, as if it might burst out. She could feel her small, full breasts straining against the skimpy lace of her bra, her nipples nudging the soft cotton of her shirt.

They swayed towards each other. All her instincts told her to step back, but she seemed rooted to the spot. Harry was bending his head, he was going to kiss her...

For a brief, mad moment Harry wondered whether shock tactics would work. He sensed that he was half-way to breaking through her cool reserve. Should he do what he wanted to do—kiss her hard and savagely, cup her small, heaving breasts in his large hands? They looked ripe and ready.

He saw in her eyes not distaste, not even the usual wariness, but uncertainty, puzzlement tinged with... fear? Dear God, don't let her be afraid of me. Play it calm, be the reassuring doctor whom she knows and respects.

He said softly, 'It's been such a lovely evening, Em. I want to give you a thank-you kiss. May I?'

A thank-you kiss! But she had thought...half hoped... Yet all he wanted was a *thank-you kiss!* For a moment she felt...betrayed, bereft, as if she had been offered something and had had it withdrawn. The hairs stood up on the back of her neck and her spine tingled as if with fright. She *was* frightened, frightened of the effect he had on her.

Then relief flooded over her. She had nothing to fear from Harry. He wanted nothing more than friendship—the rest was in her imagination. She had nearly made a colossal fool of herself by misreading the situation.

So why did she feel limp and rather empty as her heartbeat began to return to normal, the tautness drain away? Mystery!

She musn't spoil the evening. They had to get back into the teasing, happy mood in which they'd started. Her sense of humour took over. She took a deep breath, tilted her head further back, pursed up her lips theatrically and said brightly, 'You may kiss me—ready when you are.'

Smiling with equal brightness, Harry lowered his head and planted a brief, firm kiss on her pouting lips. It hadn't been the tentatively long, drawn-out, sexy one he'd planned, but it would do for now. Even with his perceptiveness, he hadn't been able to follow Emily's convoluted thoughts, but he consoled himself with the fact that she hadn't shied away from him.

It was a small victory.

Once back in the cottage, they sat at the kitchen table, drank coffee and made lists.

'You need everything from a trowel to a lawnmower before we can begin to consider buying plants,' Emily said, scribbling away busily. 'Those few tools that were left in the shed are falling to bits. They'll have to be junked.'

Undaunted, Harry said, 'Junk them. Where can we get what we need?'

'From Gardening World on the outskirts of Chellminster. They do absolutely everything in the way of gardening hardware—though we could save a bit and pick up some things second hand.'

He shook his head and waved his hand dismissively. 'No need for that. Honestly Em, I can afford whatever it takes.'

'We're talking thousands rather than hundreds if you want a greenhouse.'

He smiled. 'A greenhouse is a must. I like the idea of bringing things along from seed.' His eyes danced. 'Besides, think what I'll be able to save in the future, growing my own from scratch. It'll be a good investment. Now, when are we going shopping? What about this coming weekend when we're both off duty?'

Smiling to take the edge off her words, Emily said drily, 'Aren't you rather taking it for granted that I'll go with you? I might have other plans for my precious weekend off.'

He wasn't deceived, but smiled back at her, raising one eyebrow. 'But you haven't, have you, Em? And you *did* promise to help me with the garden. You won't renege on that, will you?'

Was it her imagination or did he sound just a trifle arrogant, sure of himself...and of her? Well, why shouldn't he? He was dead right, she'd nothing planned.

She shrugged. 'With the planting programme—not doing a complete equipping service.'

'But you will, won't you?' said Harry, leaning across the table to touch her fingers as they cradled her mug. 'Come with me?'

Her fingers tingled and she tensed them. Of course she would. It had been nothing but token resistance and they both knew it. She was longing to go on a spending spree with him, make sure he didn't get sidetracked into buying a load of unnecessary gadgets.

Really? You're sure it's not because you just want to

spend the day with him? asked her voice. She had got into the habit of ignoring her voice, and ignored it now.

She made one more token effort. 'I'll have to see what Tim's doing.'

'Going with his mates to see a film in Porthampton.'

She knew that. Tim had told her this morning. She bluffed it out, willing herself not to blush.

'Of course. I'd forgotten.'

'So we've a date?' He was smiling and there was no way she could say no. She didn't want to say no.

Her heart performed some peculiar gyrations, and her stomach churned. 'Yes, we've a date.' she said huskily.

It was a busy Friday. The town was bursting with visitors and vehicles. By mid-morning the department had already dealt with two RTAs. Miraculously, there'd been no mortalities, but there had been three severe crush injuries who had only just made it and had all been admitted to the critical care unit.

It was twelve o'clock before Emily and Jane were able to take a break. They hadn't stopped since coming on duty at seven-thirty. As tradition dictated, the juniors had been sent to the earlier breaks.

'Wow, I needed that,' said Jane, taking an unladylike slurp of coffee.

'And how,' said Emily cheerfully, doing the same.

Jane took a less urgent sip. 'Considering that we've been run off our feet since the word go, you're full of the joys of spring. Due to the fact that you're a free woman for the weekend, I presume. Doing anything interesting?'

Emily grinned. 'Yes, helping Harry buy garden equipment with a blank cheque. It's going to be fun. His ignorance of all things horticultural is abysmal.'

'He's still hooked on the good life, then?'

'Can't wait to get cracking.'

Jane gave a sly grin. 'And you and he are...?'

'Are just good friends and neighbours,' Emily said firmly. 'I told you how brilliant he's been with Tim. When I was on lates the other day he did Tim's foot and leg massage after his exercises. And they talk about football and cricket and cars, all the things that boys like. I really am grateful to him.'

'Hmm, I'm sure you are,' said Jane in her dry voice. 'Good old Harry, he sounds the ideal role model.'

'Yes, he is,' confirmed Emily simply.

'Hope you'll both have a good weekend.'

Emily beamed. 'I'm sure we will,' she said.

The afternoon was as busy as the morning had been, with an endless stream of minor accidents, but towards five o'clock, when Emily was due off duty, a thirteen-year-old boy, Keith Thompson, was brought in with serious lacerations and bruising all over his body.

It was obvious that he'd been beaten up. The ambulance had been summoned by an anonymous caller who had found him unconscious in an alleyway behind the Minster. He was conscious, though disorientated, when he arrived in Casualty.

'He came round after we'd given him a spot of oxygen,' said one of the paramedics as, with Jane's and Emily's help, they lifted the lad onto the table. 'Blood pressure's hovering around normal, pulse is feeble and erratic around seventy. He's vomited once and is complaining of pains in stomach and head—not surprising, considering the beating he's had.'

Keith slipped in and out of consciousness as Emily and Jane divested him of his torn clothing and put him into a hospital gown. He gave them his home phone number while they were attending to his superficial cuts and bruises, but refused to give any further information about his attackers.

He regained full consciousness when Harry came to examine him, but still refused to talk.

Harry said gently, when he'd finished his examination, 'Look, son, whoever did this to you must be stopped. Is it someone you know? Are you being bullied at school?'

Keith compressed his lips, his eyes looking frightened.

Harry sat on the side of the couch. 'I'm bound to report this to the police and they'll be questioning you.'

The boy turned his head away. Harry said softly, 'We're going to give you something for the pain, Keith, and admit you to the children's ward for further investigations. You may have internal injuries. We have informed your mother that you're here so she should be along soon.'

He rose and laid a comforting hand on the boy's shoulder. 'Don't be afraid to tell the truth, Keith. Bullies are at heart cowards you know.'

Half an hour later Emily was on her way home, singing Harry's praises to herself. What a warm, tactile, loving man he was. She was so looking forward to spending the day with him tomorrow.

Unexpectedly, delightfully, the weekend started with a continental breakfast on Harry's patio.

'Come and eat with me,' he called, seeing her in the garden deadheading some early roses. 'I've just put some croissants into the oven to warm, and the coffee is bubbling away.'

Emily could smell it, wafting out through the open windows and doors. It was only seven-thirty, but a glorious morning. Habit and a simmering excitement had persuaded her out of bed at seven. Why not? Tim was still sound asleep and would be for hours yet.

'Love to. Would you like a pot of home-made jam?'

'Your home-made jam?'

'My mother's. She made loads every year. I'll just pop in and get a jar.'

She chose raspberry. Her mother's neat writing on the label brought tears to her eyes. She blinked them back, before edging round the dividing wall and joining Harry at the table.

'I chose this because it was made from our own raspberries. Mother had a little vegetable and fruit plot at the bottom of the garden. It was amazing what she was able to cram into it.'

'She had the proverbial green fingers.'

'And then some.' Her voice shook a little.

Harry, picturing an older version of Emily, said gently, 'I should like to have met your mother.'

Emily smiled. 'You would have liked each other.'

It wasn't a platitude. Just as she'd felt that he and Aunt Meg would hit it off, so she was sure that Harry and her mother would have liked and respected each other. Strange how important that seemed, considering that they would never meet.

Once inside Gardening World Harry was like a child in a toy shop. They wandered around for a long time, just looking. As Emily had suspected, he was a sucker for gadgets, picking them up and examining them as carefully as he might a surgical implement. He was fascinated by any tool with a moving part.

She was thrilled to see him so absorbed and happy, free for a little while of having to make life-and-death decisions. He carried the mantle of authority with deceptively casual ease, and it wasn't until now, seeing him away from the hospital, that she appreciated what a load he carried, how tough those decisions sometimes were. Beneath the calm façade was an iron will. He might keep it well hidden, but it was there.

Strangely, this sudden insight into his character both shook her and reassured her. He was, she realised, utterly to be relied upon but never to be taken for granted.

She looked at her watch—ten o'clock. Time to call a halt to just looking. They had plenty of real shopping to do.

With a laugh she removed the extendable fruit-picker from his hands. 'You can forget that for a few years. The trees aren't even planted.'

He grinned down at her. 'Even I know that, but isn't it neat, beautifully designed?'

By lunchtime they had filled a trolley and a wheelbarrow with the basic tools which they planned to take with them in the back of the Range Rover. They found a nearby pub where they had a leisurely lunch and talked about everything under the sun.

Emily couldn't believe how relaxed she felt. She'd never felt this way with Mark. He'd been a conventional dresser, wearing dark suits and ties on duty and smartly tailored casuals off duty. On reflection, she realised that he'd *never* relaxed so consequently, neither had she. They had always both been on show, meeting the right people at the right party. His eye had always been on the professional ladder to success.

Whereas Harry… Harry had arrived where he wanted to be, both on the professional and private fronts. Workwise, he was fulfilled as head of St Luke's busy A and E unit. On the home front he was firmly putting down roots in Shalford.

She looked across at him as he sat with his elbows on the table, his large, well-kept hands nursing his pint of beer as he watched a small child playing nearby, and she wondered why he was still a bachelor. In his craggy way he was handsome, and—as he himself had put it—not short of a bob or two. So why hadn't he been snapped up? Because he hadn't wanted to be? Perhaps...

He turned his head and his eyes, full of gentle humour, met hers. 'Do I pass inspection?' he asked softly.

Emily felt her cheeks flame. 'Oh, I...I'm sorry. I was just thinking...what a successful morning we've had,' she improvised in a rush.

She knew that she hadn't deceived him. In fact, she had the odd sort of feeling that he'd half guessed at what she was thinking. But that was a nonsense.

'Yes, we have, haven't we? Now, how do you feel about greenhouse-hunting this afternoon?'

'I'm raring to go,' she said happily.

He stood up and walked round the table. He put his hands on her shoulders and dropped a kiss on the top of her head. Then he took her hand and pulled her to her feet. 'Ready?' he asked.

'Quite ready,' she replied.

CHAPTER SEVEN

EMILY leaned on the window-sill and took in several deep, satisfying breaths of early morning air. It was two sunsoaked weeks since she and Harry had gone on their buying spree. The delicate rapport that they had begun to build between them almost since his arrival in the cottage had been consolidated over that weekend into warm friendship.

It was exactly what she wanted, needed—to feel safe, unthreatened. It gave her a warm, glowing feeling to know that he was only a wall away.

She looked down on his garden, no longer bare. It couldn't yet rival her well-established herbaceous border, ablaze with midsummer colour, but marigolds, stocks, pinks and pansies made a colourful edging to the paths and well-rooted, pot-grown bushes were beginning to take hold and look as if they belonged.

The effort they had both made was already showing dividends. Although it hadn't been on the original agenda, she had spent Sunday with him, visiting a local nursery to buy bedding plants, a few starter shrubs and bags of organic fertiliser. They had spent the afternoon digging and planting.

He had looked fantastically fit and strong in the briefest of shorts, revealing powerful muscular thighs, with a thin cotton singlet enhancing his broad, lightly tanned, equally muscular shoulders. And she had experienced a little frisson of pure, unadulterated pleasure because she had been working beside him. For a fleeting moment, she had wondered what it would be like to be held in those strong arms.

With little difficulty, she had squashed the momentary desire. The relationship she had with Harry was exactly what she wanted it to be—warm, but with no sexual overtones.

Emily grinned to herself. Many of the female staff at St Luke's would have given their eye teeth to have been in her shoes and spent the weekend with Harry. He was a much sought-after eligible bachelor and they would have found it hard to believe that he and she had spent the weekend gardening.

They would probably have considered it a waste of time, time that could have been better spent, eating out at one of Chellminster's fashionable restaurants or dancing at one of the night spots in Porthampton down on the coast. Well, she was willing to concede that dancing with Harry would be fun, but...

She gave a contented little sigh. Gardening with Harry was fun too. Life was good, and she was the happiest she'd been for a very long time.

At last everything seemed to be going right for her and Tim. He continued to make steady progress as the massage with the aromatic oils and carefully regulated complementary exercises began to pay off. It was difficult to equate this generally happy youth—like anyone else he occasionally had his off days—with the sullen, unresponsive Tim of a couple of months ago.

'Pre-and post-Harry Paradine,' murmured Emily with a smile, taking another deep breath before tearing herself away from the window to get showered and dressed.

He was a constant tower of strength. He frequently joined Tim in his rather tedious exercises, now longer and more intense than initially.

Emily was becoming quite used to arriving home after

late duty or shopping and finding them both on Harry's smooth patio, methodically walking up and down with heel-to-toe, slow, deliberate steps. It was an incredibly boring exercise, designed to strengthen the muscles and soft tissues of the foot and calf and eventually straighten the inverted foot.

She put the finishing touches to the light make-up she wore and sprayed on some flowery perfume. 'That should fight off the antiseptic for all of five minutes,' she told her reflection in the mirror.

Tim was coming out of his room as she went downstairs.

'Planning anything for this evening, love?' she asked.

He pulled a face. 'Just homework and then more homework.'

'Poor old you. Well, I'll be home by half five so I'll cook you something special and creep about like a mouse so that you can concentrate. What about your exercises? When are you going to fit those in?'

'Harry said he would come round about eight and do them with me, and give me a good massage afterwards, so I'll take a break then.'

She said crisply, 'When I'm home there's no need for Harry to come round. I'm perfectly capable of doing your exercises with you *and* giving you your massage.'

Tim looked at her in astonishment. 'Well, of course you are, but you've always so much to do—washing, ironing, that sort of thing. Harry's got someone who comes in to do it for him, and he's only got to feed himself when he gets home. Honestly, Em, I don't know why you're cross. Harry thought he was doing you a favour.'

Emily was already regretting her tone. She didn't know why she had been so sharp. Surely she didn't *mind* Harry helping Tim? Of course not. No, it wasn't that, it was something to do with not being any more beholden to him than they need be. She didn't want him to feel that they were taking advantage of his kindness.

Oh, hell, she didn't know what she thought.

She shrugged and pulled a face. 'Oh, Tim, I'm sorry, I didn't mean to sound cross, I'm not—honestly. It's just that Harry's done so much for us. I don't want him to think we're taking advantage.'

Tim said, 'Don't be daft. He doesn't think that at all.' He frowned. 'In fact, I think he likes being involved with us—he more or less said so the other day.'

'Did he?'

'Yep. He said the best thing that ever happened to him was moving into number two—said the fates had been kind to him.'

Emily remembered the way his face had lit up the day he'd moved in and discovered that she lived next door. 'Really!' Her heart missed a beat or two.

'That's what he said. He thinks it's lucky that we hit it off as neighbours. And so do I. We might have had the neighbours from hell, instead of which we've got Harry. He's brilliant.'

Emily smiled and felt her cheeks heat a little. 'Well, I can't quarrel with that. And I'm sure you're dead right—he doesn't think we're taking advantage and I'm grateful to him for offering to do your massage.' Her smile widened to a grin. 'But he's not taking over my kitchen. I still intend to cook you something nice for supper. See you at half five.'

Just how wrong can you be? she thought when at four o'clock a special alert was received.

Harry called everyone together and explained in his calm way. 'There's been an explosion and a fire in the shopping precinct. Don't yet know if there are any or many casualties. We'll be informed a.s.a.p. by police. Ambulances are on the way or on standby. Meanwhile, we'll assume that there are going to be some injuries and prepare accordingly. Waiting room to be cleared of all but priority cases—tactfully, please. Dressing trolleys stacked and so on.'

He smiled his confident smile, and fleetingly Emily felt that he was smiling specifically at her. 'But you all know the drill for a disaster alert so get cracking, folks, and hang in there if things get tough. By the way, there'll be medical and nursing help drafted in. They'll all be willing but not all experienced in Casualty so, where possible, I want them working with members of our own team.' He nodded a dismissal and disappeared in the direction of his office.

'Nice touch that,' said Jane, as she and Emily hurried through to the waiting room to sort out who should stay for treatment. '"Our own team", the *crème de la crème*.'

'Yep, a real morale-booster,' Emily agreed. 'He's clever, isn't he?'

'Sure is. Not just a pretty face and a lovely guy, but clever with it.'

They needed that booster as the afternoon wore on. The stream of injured bodies seemed neverending. The critically injured were dealt with first—those with wounds causing asphyxia or threatened asphyxia through smoke inhalation who needed to be intubated, patients haemorrhaging from internal or external wounds and severe shock victims.

Emily was pleased when Jane asked her to work with Harry in one of the trauma rooms. She always enjoyed working with him and watching his calm, unhurried movements, his large hands gently examining bodies of all shapes and sizes. She was assisted by a newly qualified nurse from Men's Surgical, Karen Corbett. She was sensible and willing but a bit awed by the pace at which they had to work.

'I don't know how you keep it up,' she said, as she and Emily binned their umpteenth set of dirty aprons and gloves.

'Practice,' replied Emily, 'and it isn't always this bad. We do have our quiet moments.'

'Occasionally,' said Harry with a smile for them both as he dumped his own discarded gear into the bin. 'Press on, ladies, we're getting there.'

'He's brilliant to work with, isn't he?' whispered Karen as Harry crossed to the basin to wash his hands. 'And he's drop-dead gorgeous.'

And too old for you, Emily wanted to say, but instead agreed that he was 'brilliant'.

The next patient to be wheeled in was an elderly lady who had fallen down the stairs in the general rush to leave the building. Astonishingly, she was conscious, though very dazed. She had possible internal injuries and a badly crushed broken arm, which had been splinted by the paramedics. She was in a tremendous amount of pain and taking short, staccato breaths through her oxygen mask. The paramedics had already set up a drip to counteract shock.

'That's fine,' said Harry. He looked at the name tag that had been placed round her good wrist and smiled down at her. 'Hello, Mrs Holland. I'm Harry Paradine, the doctor in charge of Casualty. It's obvious that you've hurt your arm badly, but do you have pain anywhere else?'

'Just here, under my ribs. It hurts when I breathe in,' Mrs Holland murmured breathily through pale, stretched lips.

'Right. We'll get you into a gown so that I can examine you, but I'll give you an injection first to relieve the pain.' He flicked Emily a smile. 'Let's have 50 mg of pethidine, please, Sister.'

Emily selected the vial, checked it with Karen, drew up the liquid into the syringe and handed it to Harry together with an antiseptic swab.

'This will work quite quickly, Mrs Holland, and might make you feel drowsy, but it will give you some relief.' He swabbed her good arm. 'Just a small prick.' He pressed the swab over the small puncture. 'OK, now let's get you into a gown.'

The pethidine had begun to take effect and the patient was half dozing by the time they'd succeeded in undressing her. Taking care to move the limb as little as possible, they removed the splint and dressings that the paramedics had applied. Her right forearm from elbow to fingertips was a mess of protruding splinters of bone, blood and blue-black flesh. It must have been squashed against the stone steps when she fell.

Her wrist was badly smashed and it was impossible to find a radial pulse. Harry felt the tips of the mangled fingers and shook his head.

'Hell,' he whispered under his breath, 'nil circulation. If the orthopaedic people don't get to this soon she's going to lose that hand. All we can do is dress, pad and resplint. Emily, phone Theatres, tell them that we've got an A1 priority and I'm sending her up in a few minutes. They'd better X-ray her there. Put them in the picture. Explain that her breathing is guarded and she might have cracked or fractured ribs but there's no sign of lung puncture… Her arm is the priority. And get porters and a stretcher here at the double.'

It took time to get through to Theatres—their line was busy. So was the porters' line. By the time Emily got back to the trauma room Harry and Karen had redressed,

padded and splinted the critically damaged arm. Mrs
Holland was still breathing painfully beneath her oxygen
mask, but was looking slightly more relaxed. Clearly the
pethidine was deadening the pain.

Harry gave Emily a quick, smiling glance. 'All fixed?'
he asked.

Emily returned his smile. 'All fixed. The porters
should be here any minute and a theatre will be freed
up shortly. One of the neuro team will be available and
Julian Knight from Orthopaedics is just finishing a job.'

'Good, they must be under a hell of a lot of pressure
up there.'

'Bursting at the seams, apparently, but they're coping.'

At that moment a porter arrived with a stretcher. 'I'm
on my own,' he said. 'We're run off our feet—someone
will have to come with me.' He sounded tired but cheerful.

Harry nodded. 'Fair enough, Dave. Karen, you go and
stay with Mrs Holland till she's admitted to Theatre.
Then nip along to the staffroom and get yourself a coffee, before reporting back.'

Together the four of them lifted the drowsy patient
onto the stretcher, then she was wheeled out, with Karen
carrying the drip bag in one hand and helping to push
the trolley with the other.

As soon as they had gone, Emily started to tidy up,
binning dirty dressings and paper bed sheets and spreading fresh ones ready for the next patient.

Harry said, 'I'm going to find out what the state of
play is…won't be long.'

He was back in ten minutes. 'Things are beginning to
ease off. All the priority cases have been dealt with.
We're down to straightforward fractures and minor injuries, cuts caused through flying glass and so on. I've

told Reception we're going to take a short break. You've been on the go since seven-thirty this morning and it's now…' he glanced up at the wall clock '…nine p.m. We both need a coffee to stoke up our blood sugar or we'll be no use to anyone—come on.'

He took her hand. It felt strong and warm and comforting.

'But—'

'No buts, love. Knowing when to stop is important. We've got a few hours to go yet. And you can ring Tim—let him know that you're going to be late.'

'He knows we've got an emergency on. I left a message on the answerphone before things started to hot up here. But I'll phone and bring him up to date.'

'He's been following the news on TV,' she said a few minutes later when she joined Harry in the empty staffroom. She sank into an armchair next to his.

'Thanks.' She accepted the mug of coffee he put in her hands. 'I think he knows more about it than we do. Reporters have been outside the hospital all evening, interviewing managers. *He* told *me* that there are still a large number of casualties to be seen. He doesn't expect us home till midnight and…he'll have supper ready for us both. Says you'll be too tired to cook for yourself.'

'Well, I'm damned. Fancy him thinking of that.' Harry beamed, clearly touched.

'He thinks a lot of you, Harry, and is grateful for all that you've done for him…' Her voice trembled a little. 'And so am I. A few months ago he would never have thought of doing such a thing as having a meal ready. He was brittle and angry and at war with himself and everyone else.' Her eyes, bright with unshed tears, met his above the rim of her mug.

Harry stared into them. They were so intensely blue that he could drown in them, drown in her tears. He wanted to tell her that they were beautiful and that he was in love with her... And frighten her off for good, he warned himself drily. God, I'm getting maudlin. It's just because we're tired and a bit stressed out. He gulped down a mouthful of coffee.

'All boys of that age are against the world,' he said, almost roughly, 'and Tim had more reason than most to rebel. He would have come out of it eventually.'

Emily shook her head. 'Not without your help,' she persisted. Tears still glistened on her lashes.

Harry put his mug on the table, leaned over and with his thumbs stroked the tears away. 'Don't cry, Em,' he said softly. 'Please don't cry. I can't bear to see you unhappy.' He kept his hands cupped round her face.

She gave him a watery smile. 'Oh, Harry, I'm not unhappy—just the opposite. I'm so glad that you're around.'

He drew in a sharp breath. 'Are you? Oh, Em...'

Footsteps and voices were coming nearer the door.

He kissed her swiftly on the mouth—her lips tasted of coffee. 'We'll finish this conversation some other time.' He dropped his hands from her face and sat back in his chair just as the door opened.

It was half past eleven when with the last stragglers of the day shift, Emily and Harry left the building, leaving the night shift to carry on.

'Back to normal,' remarked Harry, as an ambulance, sirens blaring, drew up in the unloading bay.

They were about to part to walk to their respective cars—his nearby in the consultants' parking area, hers much further away in the middle of the park—when he put a hand on her arm. 'No, don't walk, jump in.'

'Bless you, kind sir, my feet are killing me,' Emily said with a chuckle.

'Hey, what's with all this jollity? You should be flat out after the day you've had. If I didn't know better, I'd say you were drunk.' Harry spun her round to face him.

Emily said lightly, 'I think I might be, drunk on adrenaline or something. I can't really explain—relief that it's all over and, though it came close several times, we didn't lose anybody. The feeling of a job well done...'

And working with you, she wanted to say, being beside you, and the fact that you kissed me... But would she have minded if he had gone further? That was the million dollar question... Her thoughts as well as her speech trailed off. In truth she really didn't know why she felt so uplifted when she should be feeling dog-tired.

Harry held her arms in his gentle grasp. He looked down at her upturned face, a ghostly yellow in the amber lighting of the car park. He wanted to pull her close and kiss her very hard, but that would be taking advantage of her strange, euphoric state, just as it would have been had she been really drunk. Her eyes were bright—too bright?

He said quietly, 'Em, I'm going to drive you home. We'll leave your car here—we're both on lates tomorrow and I'll drive you in.'

Emily stared at him for a moment, as if she hadn't heard what he had said. Then she nodded and produced a dimpled smile. 'I think that might be a good idea. I don't want to be charged with driving while under the influence of excessive adrenaline.'

Harry gave her a loving, slightly puzzled smile. 'Come on,' he said, almost lifting her into her seat. 'Let's get you home and get some food inside you.'

Both deep in thought, they drove home through the moonlit night in silence.

A lovers' moon, thought Emily, staring up at the nearly full golden disc sailing above them. Moon, June, that's how all the love songs go… She stole a glance at Harry's profile. Such a strong, masculine face. What did he think about the moon and June and lovers? She opened her mouth to ask—and shut it again. He probably hadn't noticed the moon and he certainly wouldn't be wondering about it.

He would be thinking about the emergency alert and how they'd all performed, whether there might be any improvements that could be made… Lord, I do feel odd. She closed her eyes.

Harry wasn't thinking about the emergency or about the full moon. His thoughts were concentrated entirely on Emily. He glanced down at her tenderly—her eyes were closed, her head drooping. She must be asleep. Just like a child, on a high one minute and out for the count the next.

What had brought about her out-of-character behaviour? Why the sudden euphoria, her sudden willingness to let him drive her home? If he had learned anything about her over the weeks that he had known her, it was that she was cool, detached, and very much her own woman.

Yet beneath it all she was so vulnerable. He had cracked the façade a little, chiefly because of his involvement with Tim and a little because of their combined interest in gardening, but he felt that he was nowhere near getting through to the *real* Emily. She had never confided in him. Even that weekend when they had come close she had told him very little about her childhood.

It was clear that her mother had been the loving, guiding influence in her life. Of her father she had said very little. Was he responsible for that wary expression in her eyes? Tim had been a little more forthcoming, saying very bitterly that he hadn't got on with his dad and hinting that he had a fierce temper.

He hadn't liked to press Tim, though he'd dearly have liked to know more. He felt that it would be going behind Emily's back. If she'd wanted him to know about her history she would have told him.

Tim had said something else that evening which had been a revelation—Emily had been engaged to someone whom he described as being a stuffed shirt. The impression came over of a man stiff and humourless and unpleasantly arrogant. 'He was a dead loss,' Tim had said, 'and Mum didn't like him either, though she tried not to show it. I was glad when Em packed him in—wish she had done it earlier while Mum was still alive.'

Again Harry had resisted the temptation to probe further, but it was food for thought, providing yet another possible reason for Emily keeping men at arm's length.

He looked down at her again, just as she listed sideways and her head drooped onto his shoulder. He lifted one hand from the wheel and stroked her silky black hair back from her face. It felt good to have her there. Pity they were nearly home.

She lifted her head as they turned into Harry's drive five minutes later and gave a little cry of surprise. 'Oh, Harry, I'm so sorry. I've been to sleep. How rude of me.'

He smiled. 'Not at all, you needed it. How do you feel now?'

'Fine, except for a bit of a headache, and that's probably due to lack of food. I didn't have much lunch today.'

'And nothing since then,' said Harry, as she fumbled to undo the seat belt. 'Here, let me.' He leaned across and undid the catch. As he did so his arm brushed against her breasts, and they tightened. Emily held herself rigid. His face was close to hers, smelling of soap and antiseptic—skins seemed to absorb it from the very air in Casualty—and the wispiest remains of a woody cologne.

It was very quiet in the car, lit only by the light streaming from the porch. They sat there as still and silent as statues for endless moments. Then Harry kissed her. It was a gentle, lingering kiss. She could feel the roughness of his day-long beard, chafing her chin, her cheeks. The rigidness seeped out of her. Of their own volition her arms and hands crept up around his neck. Her fingers pushed into the thick thatch of hair and pressed his head closer.

The tip of his tongue teased tentatively at her lips, pushing them gently apart. For a few moments she let him invade her mouth, then she pulled her face away from his and let her hands fall from his neck.

She shook her head and murmured in a wobbly voice, 'I'm sorry, Harry, I shouldn't have let you do that. I'm not into that sort of thing... I want us just to be friends.'

Harry straightened. 'Em, there's nothing wrong with a kiss between friends,' he said gruffly.

Emily's mouth tweaked into a slight smile. '*That* was more than just a friendly kiss. It was more the kiss of a...'

'A lover...?' Even in the dim light he could see her face flush. 'Would that be such a bad thing, Em? Knowing that someone loves you, is *in* love with you, would like to take care of you and Tim? Oh, hell, this isn't the time or place to talk about it, but let's make time tomorrow. We can't leave things up in the air like this—agreed?'

'Agreed.' She tried to sound firm, shut what he had said out of her mind. She'd think about it later.

'Good.' His voice was suddenly brisk and cheerful. 'Now let's go and do justice to this delectable feast Tim's prepared for us.'

Amazingly she was able to laugh. Extraordinary, she thought, what you can make yourself do when your heart's pounding fit to burst and your head feels as if it might explode. 'Don't expect too much. It'll just be something out of tins.'

It was tomato soup.

'With a dash of sherry in it and there's fresh coriander to sprinkle on the top,' said Tim, 'like you serve it, Em.'

There was also a basket of warm, wholemeal rolls and a plate of mixed cheeses and wine glasses on the neatly laid table.

Tim frowned. 'And I've opened a bottle of red,' he said, 'to let it breathe. I hope that's all right. I thought you'd both need a drink after the sort of day you've had.'

The sort of day we've had! Tim didn't know the half of it. Her eyes met Harry's briefly and she could see that he was thinking the same. The hours in the trauma room, patching up broken bodies, had been overshadowed by that kiss in the car and his declaration of love.

Emily gave Tim a hug. 'It's all great, love, thank you. We're both starving so start serving.'

Tim sat with them while they ate and drank, chatting away about the graphic pictures that had been shown on television.

It was a good job that he talked non-stop, Emily thought, for she couldn't contribute a single word. She was suddenly tired to the bone and could hardly lift her spoon to her mouth.

She pushed her chair back from the table and stood up. 'Sorry, must go to bed,' she mumbled. The room seemed to be going round faster and faster. Her legs buckled under her. She slid to the ground.

CHAPTER EIGHT

THE first thing Emily heard as she swam slowly up to
the surface was Harry's voice. 'It's all right, love. You
fainted but you're coming round. Stay still, don't try to
move.'

She opened her eyes. Harry's face and Tim's hung
like misty moons above her. 'Moon and June,' she gab-
bled thickly. 'Moon and June...hot.'

Harry said, 'Here, drink this, Em.' He raised her head
and pressed a cool glass to her lips.

Emily shook her head. 'No wine...'

'It's water.' He tipped the glass against her mouth. Ice
cold water trickled between her lips and down her chin.
She drank greedily. Harry was smiling down at her. The
moon face had gone.

She struggled to sit up. He put his arm around her and
she leaned against him for support.

'Sorry about that,' she muttered. 'Never fainted before.'

'Are you all right now?' Tim asked anxiously. 'You
sounded funny.'

'Fine, but a bit hot and my throat hurts.'

'I think,' said Harry, 'you've got a good old-fashioned
dose of summer flu. So it's bed and lots to drink and
aspirin for you, my girl.' As if he were lifting a feather,
he gathered her up in his arms and strode toward the
door. He paused at the foot of the stairs and spoke over
his shoulder. 'Tim, a jug of lemonade with loads of ice
in it, please.'

'OK.' Tim's voice sounded a bit shaky. He was scared.

With a tremendous effort Emily raised her head from the safe haven of Harry's shoulder. 'I'm all right, Tim,' she croaked. 'It's only a twenty-four-hour thing. I'll be over it in a day.'

Five days later Emily made her first trip downstairs, accompanied by both Harry and Tim, but only to lie on the sofa with the windows wide open, looking down the garden. Even that effort left her feeling as shaky as a leaf in the wind.

Harry tucked a rug round her legs.

Emily giggled. 'I feel like a genteel Victorian invalid.'

'Victorian you're not, but invalid you certainly are for a few more days,' he said severely. 'And don't you forget it. You're very much convalescent, something we don't give enough attention to these days. Good Lord, woman, you were delirious for a couple of days and had a roaring temperature until yesterday. You're only just on the mend.'

Tim pulled up a table and placed a jug of juice and a glass on it. 'I've got to scoot off now, Em. Neil and I are revising some notes together.'

'Of course, your mocks next week. I hope my being out for the count hasn't interfered with your work, love.'

'Nope, it hasn't a bit.' He grinned. 'In fact, there's been so much help around the house, what with Harry's cleaning lady and Aunt Meg popping in every day—not to mention Harry himself— I've hardly had to do a thing, and not having you around to nag at me has been a bonus.'

'Thanks a bunch.' Emily laughed. 'Will you be back for supper?'

'No, I'm having it at Neil's, but Harry's staying with you—it's all fixed up. That's OK, isn't it?'

'Of course, if Harry doesn't mind.'

Harry raised his eyebrows. 'I wouldn't have offered if I minded,' he said coolly.

She'd offended him or hurt him, she wasn't sure which.

When Tim had gone she pleaded, 'Harry, please don't be cross. I didn't mean that, about you minding. I don't know why I said it. It was a silly thing to say after all you've done while I've been ill.' She smiled uncertainly up at him.

The coolness fled from his eyes. His face creased into a smile. 'Yes, it was rather, when you know damn well how I feel about you. As if I would pass up an opportunity to spend an afternoon alone with you.' He pulled up a chair and sat beside her.

To her chagrin, she felt a warm flush spread over her cheeks, but she steeled herself to say what she'd wanted to say for the last five days when she'd kept waking up and finding him by her bed.

'Harry, about what happened the night I fainted…before I fainted.'

'Yes?' His eyes were tender.

'Everything's a bit hazy. I…I wasn't myself so you shouldn't read anything into what I said or…or did.'

'All we did was kiss, Em, and I asked you to marry me, and you turned me down, though you did agree to talk about it.'

He made it sound very matter-of-fact, but the kiss they'd exchanged—there had been nothing matter-of-fact about that. It had been a deep, warm, sensual, sexy kiss. Memory, which had been so elusive while she had been ill, came flooding back. She had wanted him to kiss her, and had loved the feeling of his tongue in her mouth. She had pressed his head close, had run her fingers through his crisp, chestnut hair, had wanted the kiss to go on and on.

What had possessed her? Why had she encouraged him? Led him to believe...and then drawn away from him?

She had never been kissed like that before—certainly not by Mark, who had the same detached approach to kissing as he had to his work. It hadn't bothered her. She hadn't wanted more from him and would have found the sort of kiss that Harry had given her...distasteful. She tightened her lips. How come, when she had been in love with the man? *In love!* Rubbish, she hadn't loved him any more than he had loved her.

Suddenly it was crystal clear. What a waste of all that grieving she had done when they'd parted. How could she have been such a fool? Mark was a creep, a well-dressed Adonis-like creep. Too smooth, too good-looking for words. However could she have fancied herself in love with him? In spite of the sun pouring in through the open windows and the rug over her knees, she shivered.

Harry watched the varied expressions flitting across her face, guessing at some, though not all, of what she was thinking, and asked solicitously, 'Cold?' He leaned forward to tuck the rug more firmly round her legs.

Emily shook her head.

'Then someone walked over your grave or you were thinking dire thoughts.'

'A bit of both, actually.'

'You were laying a ghost.'

Her blue eyes widened. 'How did you know that?'

'You've an expressive face. You were deep in thought for some minutes and suddenly had an attack of the shivers. In view of what we were talking about, it seemed a reasonable deduction. So, do you want to discuss it, Em—my proposal—or don't you feel up to it?

She saw the concern in his face. Her cheeks flamed into a deeper red. He *had* asked her to marry him. She remembered that now.

She said hesitantly, 'I wondered if I'd imagined it.'

'No, love, you didn't.'

'What did I say when I turned you down? I'm sorry to ask, but I was so muddled that night.'

'That you wanted us just to be friends.'

'Oh... Is that all?'

'You said you weren't ready for anything else.' He took her hand in his. 'Em, tell me, have you had a bad experience? Are you afraid of sex? I know the liberated women of today are not supposed to be, but I don't see why not.'

How like him to be so direct, to see so much, understand so much.

Emily stared down at their clasped hands and then up into his face. He was wearing the sort of expression that he did when he was trying to elicit facts from frightened patients, and yet there was something special there, just for her. His eyes, infinitely kind, tender with love, cherished her. Trust me, they said.

Could she trust him? Could she trust any man? If she had met Harry months ago, years ago, before Mark, before the accident...perhaps, in spite of her father, who'd always been there...

She said haltingly, 'Nothing happened to me directly, but my mother...' She shuddered and Harry's hand tightened round hers. 'She never said anything, but I heard things and she had bruises. If it hadn't been for us, I'm sure she would have left him. She was no doormat. But, in the event, he suddenly left and didn't come back. Mum may, in fact, have engineered it. He had a ferocious temper.'

'Tim told me,' Harry said quietly.

'Did he?' She frowned. 'I hope—'

'Don't worry. He didn't say much and I didn't pump him. He just wanted to get it off his chest one evening. You see, my love, he thinks the world of you. He doesn't want to worry you but needs to talk sometimes. Bitterness was not the only legacy from his accident. Now that he's on the mend he's grown up, skipped the worst of being a teenager. Regrets that he's given you a bad time.'

Her eyes filled with tears. Harry let go her hand and stroked them away as he had once before, with his thumbs, cupping her face with reassuring fingers. He kissed her gently, before taking his hands away.

Emily's voice wobbled as she said, 'I'm glad he confided in you, Harry.' A smile trembled on her lips. 'That's something else I have to thank you for. He's never had a man to confide in before. As you can imagine, my father was useless and so was Mark Forrester, to whom I was engaged.'

The stuffed shirt Tim had mentioned, Harry thought. 'It didn't work out, your engagement?' He knew it hadn't but didn't think it necessary to tell her that—he wanted to hear it from her own lips.

She shook her head, and a longing to pour out her feelings about Mark overcame her.

'He was horrid about Tim when my mother died. He refused to help me make a home for him—he was utterly despicable. Thought I was mad to leave a London teaching hospital for a provincial one to look after my brother. I broke off the engagement, but Tim must never know why. I don't want him to feel that I did it on his account.'

Harry said, 'Quite right.' It was hard to imagine that his lovely, sensible, level-headed Emily could have been in love with an obviously cold, conceited fish like Forrester. But women fell in love with the most unlikely of men. Was she still in love with him? It didn't seem likely, and yet...

Again he wanted to hear the truth from her own lips. 'Are you still in love with him, Em?'

'No.' An explosive no. 'Oh, Harry, I can't tell you what a wonderful relief it is to be free of him at last. He'd sort of faded, but wouldn't go quite away.'

He said, 'I'm pleased for you, Em. Now you can start getting on with the rest of your life. Think of yourself for once, do your own thing.' He stroked her black silky hair back from her face. 'Marry me, my love. Let me take care of you and Tim.'

Her fine eyebrows came together in a frown. 'I can't, Harry, I'm still not sure... What I'm trying to say is, I still want us to be friends, but...'

'I don't see why we can't be married and still be friends. Sounds to me like the perfect partnership.'

'But I'm not in love with you. At least—' her incurable need to be honest cut in '—I don't think I am. I can't love you. I'm not ready. I feel safe as I am. Besides, how do I know...?' Her frown deepened, her eyes darkened. 'Please don't make it difficult for me, Harry.'

He said gruffly, 'That's the last thing I want to do, but will you think about it, Em? Don't dismiss the idea out of hand.'

Emily nodded. 'Yes, I'll think about it.'

He stood up and dropped a kiss on her forehead. 'I won't let you down like the other men in your life. Now I'm going to make tea—scones today, courtesy of my Mrs Stubbs.'

'Your Mrs Stubbs is a dear. It was good of you to arrange for her to come in and keep things tidy while I was ill. She did more than cleaning. She helped me to the bathroom, changed my bedclothes and things like that, and always left something ready for supper. She worked a lot of extra hours. I wish you'd let me—'

'No, don't say it, Emily. I won't accept a penny. It's the very least I can do, make sure that you're properly looked after. You won't marry me but don't deny me that privilege as a friend. After all, what are friends for? And she's coming in each day until you're fit enough to return to work. Now, love, relax while I get the tea.'

A while ago, she thought, listening to Harry pottering around in the kitchen, I would have sent him packing. Wouldn't have allowed him to be so high-handed and...managing. So what's changed? Why don't I mind? In fact, why do I rather like him being bossy?

She still hadn't reached any answers when he returned a little later with a laden teatray.

It was to be another week before her GP would allow her to return to work.

'You've had a particularly bad dose of flu,' he said, 'and it's left you a bit chesty. Make the most of this glorious weather. Whack on the sunscreen, sit outside and soak up the fresh air.'

She didn't always sit for, although she felt limp and exhausted, she was also restless, mulling over what Harry had said. She would wander round deadheading the roses, which, in the heat, were blossoming and dying in a few days.

But in the quiet of the afternoons after Mrs Stubbs had left she would crash out on the lounger to doze and dream. Often her dreams were about Harry. Once she dreamed that she was marrying him in the pretty little local church. Gorgeously gowned, she sailed down the aisle on Tim's arm, and Tim was striding along with not a hint of a limp.

Harry was waiting at the altar, looking incredibly sexy in his gardening shorts and an elegant silk T-shirt with I LOVE EMILY on it, topped off with a bow tie. She woke, giggling, which brought on a spluttering coughing attack, and was left wondering, when she stopped coughing, if the dream had any significance.

Was it wishful thinking? Tim, walking without a limp—a possibility, but still some way off—and his dream of one day being back in the football team a still more remote possibility. And marriage to Harry! Was she mocking it by dressing him as she had? Or was her subconscious telling her to marry him, make love to him, have sex with him? *No*, she didn't want that...

Perhaps she was undersexed or indifferent to sex? Perhaps Mark's coldness had rubbed off onto her? No, that wasn't true, she thought, recalling Harry's kiss and her response to it. She'd had an instinctive dull ache in her guts, a pent-up longing that only his touch would release. So was it because she didn't want to upset the safety and security of his friendship? Was she simply afraid to take this final step committing herself to the love and care of one man?

He'd said that he loved her—but Mark, in his detached fashion, had declared his love, and look how that had turned out. True, she was attracted to Harry... She gave a snort of derision. 'Attracted' was a stupid milk-and-water sort of word for what she felt for Harry. But was that because she was so grateful to him for what he'd done for Tim? Could she trust this feeling that she had for him? Was it love or just hormones, clamouring for attention?

Being in love was what? Wanting to be with someone

all the time, having one's heart turn over at the sound of that someone's voice. Wanting to cherish and be cherished in return. Having that someone always on one's mind, wanting to share, just be together.

Well, her heart did do some funny acrobatics sometimes, and she couldn't get Harry out of her mind and they had been very happy, sharing the gardening!

Was she in love with him—should she marry him? And what about Tim in all this? He was the most important factor. He liked Harry, admired him, but no way would he want him as a brother-in-law—would he?

Her thoughts invariably ended on this note. Perhaps only time would provide the answers. Meanwhile, she would continue to enjoy Harry's unwavering friendship and give what she could in return.

Harry, pulling rank for the first time in his career, was, short of emergencies, doing early shifts so that he was home most evenings to help Tim with his exercises and massage. He also watered both gardens, a long, tedious job as there was a hosepipe ban in force, flatly refusing to allow Emily to lift a bucket or watering-can.

Neither would he let Tim help, considering that he had enough to do, preparing for the next day's exams and getting through his exercise massage session. He never missed working out with Tim, knowing that sharing the session with him boosted his morale.

As did the ten-minute exercise of pushing a football back and forth, which Bob Keefe had now introduced into his schedule. It was a long way from the real thing but gave Tim an enormous amount of pleasure, though he found it tiring and was warned not to exceed the ten minutes. Harry enjoyed it too, but, added to the other exercises and the massage, it took a forty-minute slice out of the evening.

Not that he minded. To see Tim make progress and pleasing Emily was reward enough.

In fact, pleasing Emily became—apart from his work when, by making a supreme effort, he shut her firmly out of his mind—his prime concern.

He longed to make her his wife so that he could cherish and care for her. On an earthy, physical level he literally ached, loin-deep, to make love to her. To cup her soft breasts in his hands, to feel her thighs and her abdomen mould themselves to his. To hold her, and gently, gently, thrust into her so as not to frighten her, not to hurt her.

Emily was precious, the love of his life. He wanted to make up to her for the fear that her father had caused her, for the death of her beloved mother. Most of all, he wanted to make up to her for the way that that cold, slimy toad, Forrester, had treated her. He longed to teach her the value of true love.

So he daydreamed, and occasionally night-dreamed, when Emily would appear fugitively as he slept. Waking up one morning, frustrated as he tried to catch her elusive image and the substance of his dream, which remained just out of reach, he came to a decision. He would step up his pursuit of the real Emily, break through the barriers, allay her fears—whatever it took.

'I shall woo her,' he told his bedroom walls, 'like an old-fashioned Victorian, quietly and persistently. We will go out and about, be seen as an item, become a couple. That'll please the grapevine gossips, who've probably already had us in bed together.'

He sighed heavily as he got out of bed and made for the bathroom. 'Would that we had,' he muttered, as he stood under the shower. Visibly aware that his body agreed with him, he turned the shower on cold, full blast.

Coming home early one afternoon, he found Emily, her straw hat tipped over her face, sound asleep on the sun lounger in the dappled shade of the ancient apple tree that graced her lawn. With his heart knocking against his ribs, he stood watching her for some minutes.

She was wearing a short, loose dress of filmy silk, blue as her eyes, that showed off her long, lightly tanned legs. Her breasts rose and fell rhythmically against the soft material. Her golden arms were flung up above her head. She looked fabulous, abandoned, yet innocent and vulnerable at the same time.

Harry sucked in his breath. He wanted to stroke her sun-warmed thighs, lay his head on the soft mounds of her breasts, feel their gentle rise and fall, tease her nipples, listen to her heartbeat...

With a muttered oath he turned, pushed his way through the lavender hedge and made for his kitchen. It was either a cold beer or a cold shower. He compromised on the shower but tore off his tie, unbuttoned his shirt to the waist and sloshed his face and torso with cold water. Then he fished out a can of beer from the fridge and returned to the garden.

He sat down on the grass, sipping his beer, idly turning the pages of a magazine but not seeing anything of the printed page. He emptied his glass and stretched out flat to ease his aching back. Perchance to dream of Emily, he thought wryly as he felt his eyelids drooping.

A blessedly cool breeze was fanning his face. He opened his eyes to find Emily leaning over the edge of the lounger, fanning him with her straw hat. Her eyes glittered down at him. He reached up and caught her hand in mid-swing, removed the hat from her fingers and lifted his head so that he could kiss the pale inside of her wrist.

The gesture had been automatic. He half expected her to pull her hand away, but she didn't.

'Hi,' she said softly. 'You looked so hot and so tired.' Her eyes were now gentle, concerned. 'Had a busy day?'

He let go of her hand and hauled himself up into a sitting position. 'You could say that. A nasty RTA this morning, involving a minibus taking disabled kids to school.'

'Oh, no. Were there any…?' She couldn't bring herself to say 'fatalities'.

He knew what she was asking. 'Not amongst the kids, but the driver was D.O.A. and an elderly couple in another car were in a pretty bad way. But we resuscitated them and sent them up to Intensive Care. I phoned before I left, and they're both holding their own. The kids mostly got away with cuts and bruises, though some of them were quite severe. There were several fractures, but uncomplicated, and one little girl was concussed. We're keeping her in overnight for obs.'

He frowned. 'But you know how it is with kids—it gets to you somehow. And because these kids were disabled it seemed worse. There was one lad, cerebral palsy, slow in speech and movement but bright as a button. He needed stitches in his cheek—he'd been cut by flying glass. He didn't flinch. Just said laconically, with a wobbly grin, that he hoped I was making a neat job of it as he couldn't afford a scar, it might spoil his looks. He was wearing thick specs and had terrible uneven teeth.'

Harry stood up and gave Emily a grim, tight smile. 'Poor little guy, he really got to me. I wished I could have done more for him—for his palsy and his buck teeth and his bad sight.'

Emily swung her legs round and sat up. The lounger rocked. She pointed to the grass in front of her. 'Sit

down there,' she said, in a voice that dared him to argue.
'You're all tensed up. I'm going to give your neck and
shoulders a massage, help you unwind. I'm no Bob
Keefe, but I've had a lot of practice.'

Obediently he sat down cross-legged in front of her.
She pushed his shirt down over his shoulders. He slipped
his arms out of the sleeves and pushed it down to his
waist.

'That's right. Now relax.'

Relax! With her parted thighs pressed against his bare
flesh? Close your eyes and think of England, he told
himself.

Amazingly he *did* relax as she stroked and kneaded
along the line of his collar-bone, down his upper arms,
deep into his aching biceps, up his neck and into his
hairline. Then she went up and down his spine with her
thumbs and across the flat plane of his scapula with the
heels of her hands. He could feel the knotted muscles
unravelling.

After twenty minutes he was beginning to nod off. He
jerked himself awake and murmured, 'You must stop
now, Em, you'll wear yourself out.'

Emily gave his broad, muscular shoulders a final
stroke. 'There—do you feel less tense?' She smoothed
his ruffled hair. She was almost tempted to kiss the top
of his head. He looked like a little boy—well, his untidy
head did, but not the rest of him, she thought, a little
tremor of awareness of his virility and sheer masculine
beauty trickling through her.

Harry shrugged himself back into his shirt but left it
unbuttoned. He stood up in one easy, fluid movement
and turned to face her. He stared down at her upturned
face. Her eyes, fringed by black silky lashes, were glowing—like real sapphires, he thought. She must have a

sapphire engagement ring, a cluster of small stones, not one big one—her hands are too small.

She was smiling her lovely dimpling smile, waiting for his answer.

He lifted her hands from her lap and pulled her to her feet.

'Harry...?' her voice, questioning, was soft and wavery. She slipped her hands out of his and placed her palms flat on his chest. Her fingers slid between the curling hairs of gold-tinted chestnut.

His heart thundered, skipped a few beats. Did she have any idea what she was doing to him? And what about her? He'd felt her tremble, he hadn't imagined it. She'd enjoyed giving him that massage—the way she had stroked and pummelled had told him that. Was the time right to start putting on a little pressure, break through the barrier?

God, he was tired of all this pussyfooting around. He wanted her for his wife, his lover, and all his instincts told him that she wanted him. *But.* It was a hell of a big but. How should he go about it? What else must he do to convince her that he would never leave her high and dry as the toad Forrester had done? Or beat her up as her father had apparently beaten up her mother?

Not that she would suspect him of the latter. But had she been so badly shattered by her ex-fiancé's behaviour that even though she'd laid his ghost she was still afraid of it happening again? That had to be why she was reluctant to make a commitment.

Her eyes were puzzled, anxious. 'Harry, are you all right?'

He forced a smile. 'I'm fine,' he lied. He lifted her hands from his chest and folded them between his own.

He looked into her puzzled eyes. 'No, that's not quite true—I'm worried about you, Em.'

'But I'm almost back to normal. I'll be back at work in a few days' time.'

He shook his head. 'Oh, you're OK physically.'

'I don't follow you—what else is there for you to worry about?'

'Your emotional well-being.' His voice was as dry as dust.

She tried to pull her hands from his but he refused to release them. 'Please, let me go.'

'Not until you've answered one question, Em.'

Emily licked her lips. 'And what's that?' she whispered.

'Do you love me?'

Did she love him? Is that what everything added up to? The happy hours spent gardening, at work, sharing a meal, a glass of wine, that one passionate kiss, those occasions when she had felt drawn to him by a silken thread. If it was love, did she love him enough to trust him? She'd only known him a couple of months and she had sworn *never* to trust a man again.

She raised her eyes to meet his and said in a huskier than usual voice, 'Honestly, I'm not sure, Harry.'

He dropped her hands.

'Do you believe that I love you and want to care for you and Tim?'

'Yes.' She would have liked to embroider it by listing all the things he had done for her and Tim, but she knew that wasn't what he wanted to hear. It was her love, not gratitude, that he wanted.

'Then why not take a chance on my love being enough for both of us? We've got such a lot going for us. And I believe you do love me. You just haven't realised it yet.'

He put his hands on her shoulders, drew her close, bent his head and kissed her on her forehead, her nose and her lips. 'Come on, let's go and get tea ready. Tim'll be home soon and he'll be starving as usual.'

Emily joined in the pretence that everything was back to normal. 'Good. I made a chocolate cake this morning, my first stint in the kitchen since—'

'Since the flu bug struck,' said Harry.

And you came like a white knight to the rescue, thought Emily, her eyes glittering with held back tears as she followed him towards the kitchen. If only I had the guts to love you as a white knight should be loved. She heaved a sigh. Well, miracles do happen. Perhaps I will one day.

By Monday Emily was back on duty and in the thick of another RTA involving a small busload of retired people on a day out. Jane appointed her triage nurse, sorting out the seriously injured from the less wounded. Her job was to get brief medical details from the paramedics and tag patients with an identification bracelet, before sending them through to the trauma room or cubicles for treatment.

After a quick initial tour of inspection around the wheelchairs and stretchers she was able to confirm that most of the injured, though shocked, were suffering only minor cuts and bruises, to be dealt with as soon as possible but not as a matter of extreme urgency.

Of the twelve elderly people injured, two were in need of urgent attention. A Mrs Irene Watts, sixty-five, as well being badly cut by broken glass was in the throes of an acute asthma attack triggered by shock, and a ninety-year-old man, Alfred Gibson, was bleeding profusely from a head wound, in spite of the pressure pad that had been applied. He was also experiencing a great deal of pain from a below-knee fracture, which had been splinted by the paramedics.

Mrs Watts was cyanosed, the ring of blue round her mouth darkening as she fought for breath. She was too disorientated to use her nebuliser, and her condition was critical.

She and Mr Gibson were both whisked off for immediate attention from Harry and Guy, who were manning the trauma room.

Jonathan Jones, assisted by a house officer who had been drafted in to help, was taking care of the cubicles.

Emily remembered Harry's remark about the vulnerability of the young as she supervised the transfer to the cubicles of those next in need of treatment. It was true of the old, too, she thought as she helped lift a frail elderly lady from the stretcher to the bed who, as well as cuts to her face, had a broken ankle.

Just as Harry had been touched by the bright small boy with cerebral palsy so she was touched by Mrs Grace Sanderson, aged eighty-six. Mrs Sanderson, in spite of torn stockings and the blood which had stained the front of her snow-white hair and splashed onto her pale blue suit, still managed to look dignified and even produced a smile of sorts.

She reminded Emily a little of her mother or Great Aunt Meg. They had style and dignity and could smile in the face of adversity, just as Harry's little palsied boy had smiled.

Emily and Beth undressed Mrs Sanderson and got her into a hospital gown. Although she was clearly in pain, she raised her good leg an inch or two off the bed, pulled a face and said wryly, 'Talk about pride going before a fall. I've always been proud of my ankles. I was a dancer once, you know, but I'm afraid my left one will never be the same again—no good for the front row of the chorus.'

Beth said in a tone of admiration, 'You've got gorgeous legs. I hope mine are as good as yours when I'm your age.'

Emily, hoping she was not being too optimistic, gave the gallant old lady a smile and said encouragingly, 'We've got the best orthopaedic surgeons in the county. In a few months you'll have a beautiful matching pair again.'

Mrs Sanderson, smiling faintly, leaned back against her pillows. 'Well, just as long as they can weld me together so that I can totter to the shops I'll be satisfied.'

The encounter with Mrs Sanderson cheered Emily for the rest of the day, helping her to overcome the fatigue that threatened to overwhelm her as she came towards the end of her duty period.

After all the attention he had given her while she had been ill, she missed not seeing and talking to Harry. She felt physically and emotionally drained.

He'd been busy in the trauma room all day. A succession of critically ill patients needing his attention had followed the RTA with which the day had started. There'd been two myocardial infarctions in quick succession, an attempted suicide involving a cut jugular vein and gallons of blood, and a particularly nasty abdominal and chest stabbing.

Amazingly, he hadn't lost anybody.

While he'd been engaged in his life-and-death dramas Emily had worked her way steadily through the more mundane stuff of giving injections, dressing ulcers and stitching up superficial wounds.

They met eventually outside his office as she was going off at three o'clock. His eyes lit up when he saw her.

Emily was about to remark how tired he looked when he said, 'Oh, Em, you look so tired. Are you sure you haven't overdone it on your first day back?'

She ignored the remark and said, 'You look tired too.'

He grinned his lovely lopsided grin that did such wonderful things to his craggy face.

He drew in a deep breath and thumped his vast chest. 'Me Tarzan—you Jane. You've been ill, love, I'm A1 fit.' His warm hand rested briefly on her shoulder. 'Promise me you'll go home and rest. I'll be over later to see to Tim's massage.'

Emily nodded. She felt suddenly weak and tearful and was glad to be told what to do. 'Thank you, Harry.'

His eyes cherished her. 'Drive carefully.'

'Will do.'

CHAPTER NINE

JUNE merged into July without a break in the weather. Each day dawned blue, gold and cloudless, competing, said the weather men, with the long, hot summer of 1976. The hosepipe ban was extended to more southern counties and everyone was urged to save water.

Like all good gardeners, Emily and Harry saved bathwater and every bowlful used in the kitchen to keep their precious plants from wilting. If either of them were working late they fetched and carried endless cans and buckets to keep both gardens flourishing.

To Harry's satisfaction, this mutual dependence brought them quite naturally closer together. Emily, who had been for a short while rather uptight and wary, following the intimate episode in the garden when they had both opened their hearts, slowly began to relax again.

By mid-July they were almost, but not quite, back to where they had been before that confrontation had taken place. Not quite because Harry refused to let them slip back too far. Whether Emily liked it or not, things had subtly changed that day and they were both aware of it.

He began his policy of wooing her more openly, as he had vowed to himself he would. For openers he asked her to help him with the delayed housewarming party that he'd promised to throw for the A and E staff and other friends.

'We could open up both gardens—there'll be quite a crowd. We've talked for ages about removing that end lavender bush to make it easier to get round the fence.

Let's do it, Em, it'll be fun, a sort of joint do. After all, you haven't had a housewarming either.'

They were sitting in the empty staffroom, snatching a late coffee. Unusually for Harry, he had opted to join her instead of taking his mug through to his office and doing his paperwork. Not that they had many minutes as the waiting room was chock-a-block.

Emily, startled by the idea, was cautious. 'Oh, I don't know if it's a good idea, Harry. I don't know any of your friends, apart from Casualty staff. It might look a bit pushy, give people the wrong idea.'

'And what idea is that?' he asked, his eyes twinkling.

Emily couldn't stop herself blushing. 'You know jolly well what I mean. People will think—'

'That we're a couple?'

Her cheeks flamed hotter. 'Something like that.' Her voice was a few decibels huskier than usual. She stared into her coffee.

He said, very, very softly, 'Would that be such a bad thing, Em?' Damn, he hadn't meant to get heavy. He'd meant to sound casual, to tease her into co-hosting the party so that people got used to seeing them together, instead of which his tone of voice had given him away, underlining his feelings for her.

She lifted her head her blue eyes, which were bold and sparkling. She was angry. 'But you know that we're *not* a couple, Harry.' It was a challenge, a reminder that this was something already settled between them.

He looked back at her unflinchingly. Meet one challenge with another. 'We're good friends and colleagues and neighbours. It's the most natural thing in the world that we should join forces. If other people want to read more into it than that, let them. I expect the hospital grapevine has already done that, anyway.' This time he made his voice clipped, matter-of-fact.

There was a moment's silence then, to his relief, Emily nodded and said slowly, 'Yes, I dare say you're right. I shouldn't mind about these things. Sorry if I jumped down your throat. After all, *we* know what the score is, don't we, Harry?' she added with saccharine sweetness.

So there was a sting in the tail, and it was her turn to twinkle.

Harry smiled. 'Touché. I deserved that, but I'm not ashamed of my feelings, Em.' He added rather sadly, 'I wish we were a couple, in every sense of the word.'

The sing-song wailing of a siren, signalling an approaching ambulance, cut off the need for her to make any reply and Harry, it seemed, had no wish to pursue the conversation. 'We might as well take this one,' he said, leading the way towards the unloading bay.

'Heatstroke,' said Tom, one of the paramedics, as they unloaded the young male patient onto the wheeled stretcher. 'Collapsed when jogging. He's been drifting in and out of consciousness. Oxygen started immediately we arrived on the scene. Has complained of nausea, headache and stomach cramps. Rectal temp. hovering around 40 C. IV saline started, slow infusion to avoid pulmonary oedema. Fluids given orally when possible. We've sponged him a couple of times and played the fan over him.'

'Know what his name is?' asked Harry as they transferred him onto the cubicle couch.'

'John Summers.'

'OK, chaps, thanks. We'll take it from here.' He bent over the patient. 'John, can you hear me?'

John mumbled incoherently.

Harry said close to his ear, 'John, you collapsed with heatstroke and you're in hospital. Your temperature's very high so Nurse is going to sponge you off, which will help bring it down, and I'm going to put a catheter into your bladder so that we can check how much urine you pass.'

John moaned and tried to drag off the oxygen mask. Emily held it in position and told him in firm, kind tones that he must leave it alone, reflecting as she did so that it was always difficult dealing with semi-conscious patients. You could never be sure how much they heard or understood.

In all, it took forty minutes to get his rectal temperature down to a safe 39 C. To speed up the process Harry introduced an antipyretic into the drip. A few minutes later he was called away to attend to a frightened child who had been badly bitten by a dog, leaving Emily to carry on with her tepid sponging and write up the patient's charts.

John regained full consciousness after twenty minutes and Emily explained to him all over again what had happened to him and what was being done to help him recover. She also read him the riot act about running in the hot sun without taking water or salt tablets with him.

'If it hadn't been for a passerby immediately summoning an ambulance, you might have had real problems,' she said with some severity to ram the lesson home. Then, a little more mildly, she asked if there was anyone she could contact for him who would be able to take him home when he was fit to be discharged.

'My girlfriend, Maggie,' he replied croakily. Emily gave him another drink of iced, lightly salinated water. 'You can get her at her office, the Chellminster Building Society. She's going to be mad at me—she's been on at me about running in the heat.'

'She's a sensible girl, you should have listened to her.'

'Don't worry. I will in future. I won't repeat this sort of caper again in a hurry. I thought I was going to die.'

He pulled a face. 'So, what's the drill now, Nurse? How long do you think I will have to stay put?'

'Dr Paradine will decide that, but about another hour or so, I should think, to make sure that your temperature is stable and your fluid intake and output is something like normal. You must drink plenty when you get home to continue to make up for the fluids you've lost, and lay off the running for a few days. Come back at once or call your GP if the cramps or any other symptoms return.'

John managed a slight grin. 'You've got a nice line in after-sales pitch,' he said.

'All part of the service.' Emily laughed.

The rest of the day flashed past as an endless stream of patients arrived in Casualty, some under their own steam and some by ambulance. As fast as one patient was sent home or admitted to a bed, if one was available, or parked in a cubicle while awaiting a bed, another customer joined the queue.

Emily was relieved to find that her path didn't cross Harry's as the afternoon wore on. She wasn't quite sure how to handle this housewarming party idea, she mused as she waited for an elderly man, hobbling painfully with sticks, to follow her to a cubicle. On the face of it Harry was right. It made sense to use both gardens, and people would talk anyway, as he'd pointed out—probably already were.

She squashed her personal thoughts and smiled at the old gentleman who had reached the cubicle at last. 'You should have let me get you a wheelchair, Mr Carter,' she said, feeling guilty because she hadn't insisted, though he had been adamant that he wanted to walk. She steered him across to the couch and helped him up onto it. He could barely make it.

His face was contorted with pain. 'Don't like to give in to these bloody hips,' he wheezed. 'Gotta keep going till I get replacements.'

It was the same old story. Emily's heart went out to the frail, courageous old man. 'Have you been waiting long?' she asked softly.

'Eighteen months.'

Poor old chap. He'll be dead before he moves to the top of the list, she thought.

'I'm sorry.' She looked at the note she'd taken from the board. 'But you've come in today because you've hurt your knee.'

'That's right. Had a fall at home this morning. My doc can't see me till tomorrow night but it's giving me hell. Thought you could give me something for the pain. My regular painkillers don't seem to do anything for it— need something stronger.'

'How did you get here?'

'By taxi.'

'Why on earth didn't you phone for an ambulance? You'd have been seen quicker.'

'Didn't want to make a drama out of it.'

Emily sighed. It was amazing how people treated the health service. Some took advantage and some, like the elderly Mr Carter, went out of their way to avoid asking for help.

'Right, well, I'll get you seen by a doctor as soon as I've got you undressed and into a gown.'

It took ten minutes to divest Mr Carter of his layers of clothes.

Harry was the first doctor she found who was free. He accompanied her back to the cubicle and introduced himself to the patient in his courteous manner. Very gently he examined the grossly swollen knee.

'I'm going to get this X-rayed, Mr Carter,' he explained. 'I think it's more than just badly bruised.'

He ordered a mobile X-ray to avoid moving the patient more than necessary. While they were waiting for the result to come through Harry gave him an injection of pethidine to relieve the pain.

He was right about the injury to the knee. 'You've got a tiny hairline fracture at the bottom of the femur where it hinges into the knee joint,' he explained to Mr Carter in layman's language, 'so I'm going to admit you to the orthopaedic ward for observation and treatment.'

The old man's face fell. 'Can't you strap it up or something and let me go home? Have to keep moving or I'll seize up.'

Harry squeezed his shoulder and grinned. 'Afraid not. But it may not be all bad news. There's a good chance that the orthopaedic consultant will decide, in view of what's happened, to do your hip replacement on that side while you're in. We'll see what he has to say.'

Which means, Emily thought, that you're going to put in a good word for the old boy. She could have hugged him. He was the kindest man in the world. His responsibility toward his patients officially finished when they were discharged from the department, but he didn't see it that way. He cared what happened to them afterwards. She swallowed a lump which had suddenly materialised in her throat.

Mr Carter grabbed Harry's hand, and his eyes glistened. 'Doctor, if I get my hip done, this fall would be the best thing that has ever happened to me.'

'You understand it's not definite, Mr Carter. It'll be up to Mr Swayley and his team.'

'Understood, Doctor, and thanks.'

Harry shrugged. 'Nothing to thank me for, old chap. I've just taken a couple of nice pictures of your knee

and given you a jab.' He looked at his watch. 'Well,
duty calls. I've got to be off. Goodbye, Mr Carter, and
good luck.' With a wide smile and a nod to Emily he
was gone.

Emily didn't see any more of Harry that day. He was
giving a lecture at Porthampton University Hospital and
had warned her that he wouldn't be back until late. She
watered both gardens and was glad that Tim insisted on
helping her. He wasn't so hard pressed these days. With
his mocks and the term nearly over, he had plenty of
free time.

Later, when she was massaging his leg after he had
done his exercises, she told him of Harry's idea for a
housewarming party.

'I think it's a brill idea. You never have people in,
except for Aunt Meg. It'll be fun for you.'

Emily forbore to mention that she hadn't had people
in, not even old schoolfriends with whom she'd kept in
touch, because for months after the accident he hadn't
wanted to see anyone. Not that she'd been keen. He'd
been so rude and unpredictable in those days. Now that
he was the new, made-over Tim, those days seemed a
lifetime ago.

It was too hot to sleep. Emily lay on her bed and thought
about Harry and listened for his return. She couldn't get
his image out of her mind. He had practically proposed
to her again today. She recalled his deep, sad voice, saying passionately, 'I wish we were a couple, in every
sense of the word.' It had been full of longing.

She closed her eyes but his dear face floated behind
her lids. That lovely mobile mouth that smiled so readily, those tender brown eyes...

'Oh, Harry, my love.' The murmured words hung, disembodied in the darkness. *No*—not her love. Not possible. It wouldn't do. There was Tim to think of.

She sat up and turned on her bedside lamp—might as well read for a bit. The words danced before her eyes and didn't make sense. She drew her legs up into the foetal position, rolled on her side and tried to ignore the ache in the pit of her belly and the painful, uneven beating of her heart.

Harry returned just before midnight. She heard his car come up the lane and switched off the light before he turned into the drive. Perhaps now she could sleep.

Emily slept, she thought, deep and dreamlessly, but when she woke in the morning it was to find the pillow wet with tears. It was as if something momentous had happened, but she didn't know what…only that it had to do with Harry and somehow, in spite of the tearstains, it boded well and she felt elated. Weird!

That evening, sitting on Harry's patio, they discussed the housewarming party. They had finished the watering and were sipping ice cold white wine spritzers. Notwithstanding the tear-wet pillow and curious unremembered dream, Emily felt relaxed and happy in his presence, not embarrassed, as she had thought she might.

He was nursing his glass in his strong fingers, taking small, neat sips of the crystal clear liquid and rolling it round in his mouth like a wine taster, before tilting back his head and letting it trickle down his throat. With each swallow his Adam's apple moved up and down beneath the tanned skin. He looked incredibly sexy, thought Emily, a sudden longing to kiss the mobile Adam's apple overtaking her.

She looked away hastily and concentrated on her own wine. 'So, when are we going to have this shindig?' she asked.

'The Saturday after next. We've both got the weekend off.'

'You've been checking up on me again.'

'Of course, what else?' he said, unabashed. 'I always check the nursing roster to see what your duties are. Should you forget to tell me, I like to know where you are or are going to be.' He waved a nonchalant hand at the garden. 'The watering and Tim's physio…'

He doesn't really mean that, thought Emily, it's code for 'I love you'. Not that he needed a code. Over the past weeks he'd made no bones about how he felt about her.

His eyes, dark liquid brown pools, meshed with hers. The silken cord was there, pulling them closer. The birds stopped singing. A lone bee stopped buzzing. Emily stopped breathing. The world stood still—there was nothing but those dark liquid pools.

There was a pain in her chest. She took in a long, shuddering breath. Harry was saying something—she could see his lips moving. He was standing up, coming round the table. She closed her eyes.

His voice came over faintly, thick and low, urgent.

'Em, are you all right?' He bent over her and removed her glass from her nerveless hands. He placed his fingers on her pulse. 'You're as white as a sheet. You're not going to faint on me again, are you?'

She shook her head—not a good idea. The world spun for a moment. 'Not on your life, that was a one-off.' She produced a shaky smile and hoped that it looked more natural than it felt. She even managed a casual shrug. 'I think I stopped breathing for a moment, and it's so hot and airless.' Would he accept that?

Harry took his fingers from her wrist and said softly, 'Yes, it is. I almost stopped breathing myself.'

He knew. Emily, keeping her eyes glued to her glass, which she had picked up again, failed to see the flare of love and hope in his.

She took a sip of wine and attempted briskness. 'Now, about this party, we'll have to get cracking and cooking if we're to be ready by Saturday week.'

'Mrs Stubbs said she'd help, both with the cooking and on the night. We should talk numbers first. Let's draw up a list— I'll fetch paper and pencils.'

In spite of her reservations about the party and the direction that her relationship with Harry seemed to be taking, Emily found herself enjoying the busy whirl of the next ten days. Trawling the supermarket together for basic party food or visiting the upmarket delicatessen for luxury items was fun.

Fun, she privately admitted, because they shopped as a couple. Not perhaps quite the couple Harry wanted them to be, but heading in that direction. Harry made no secret about how he felt about her. In the crowded supermarket he would take her hand or put his arm about her waist in a possessive sort of fashion, as if the crowds might crush her. And she revelled in it, loved the feeling of being cherished and protected.

Just as casually, he had taken to brushing a kiss across her cheek, or sometimes her lips, when they parted. But there were no repeats of the soul-searching eye contact episode, perhaps because they both went out of their way to avoid it.

Resolutely, she refused to analyse her feelings in too great a depth, determined for the time being to give herself up to enjoying the moment and his company.

Both the kitchens of the cottages were full of delicious aromas. In number two, Mrs Stubbs turned out stacks of pies and pastries to go into the freezer, and Emily did the same in number one.

'Mmm, smells like Christmas,' said Tim, on the evening before the party, pinching a mushroom-and-bacon-filled vol-au-vent from the tray that had just come out of the oven. 'Want any help, Em?'

Emily laughed. 'Not that sort of help, thanks, but you can do some washing up.'

Tim groaned but filled the bowl and started on the pile of dishes. 'I'm glad you've invited Neil's parents,' he said. 'They're looking forward to it.'

'It seems a good way of getting to know them better. They've been good, having you round when I've been on duty. Are you sure you and Neil will be OK at his house? You're welcome to join in here if you want to.'

'Oh, Em! Of course we'll be OK. We're getting out a couple of videos, we'll have a brill evening—but it would be great if I could take some party grub with me. Mrs Makepiece is a nice lady, but her cooking's a bit basic, not like yours. Harry says that you cook like a dream, though you won't admit it.'

Emily went pink. Her heart pitter-pattered. She laughed airily. 'Does he?' She busied herself, lifting another tray from the oven. 'Anyway, I think some ''party grub'' can be managed. I'll sort you out some goodies in the morning.'

Tim slanted her a sideways look. 'You're ever so happy these days, Em. Is it because of Harry? Do you fancy him?'

All sorts of alarm bells rang. Did he sound bothered by the idea? She glanced at his profile. He looked serious. This was the sort of question she'd hoped to avoid. How could she tell if he would mind if she said that she 'fancied' Harry? Did he want her to deny it? Was he afraid that she and Harry…?

She avoided a direct answer. 'These last few days have been fun, preparing for the party. Harry's a good friend to have and good company, and you were right about entertaining. I should do more of it. I will in the future.'

Tim nodded. His face gave nothing away. 'Yeah, sounds like a good idea.'

And with that, she thought, I'll have to be content.

The party went with a swing from the word go. It was another lovely summer's night, warm and sultry. Harry and Tim had rigged fairy lights along the fences and in the apple tree and, via an extension cable, Harry's music centre played soft, sweet music—a perfect background to conversation or to dance to.

Everyone they had invited appeared to have come and both gardens were thronged with people. All the hired tables and chairs, scattered about the lawns, were filled.

Emily and Harry spent the first couple of hours separately doing the rounds, making sure that everyone was introduced and glasses and plates were kept filled. But at ten o'clock, with the sun well and truly set, dusk giving way to a star-dusted purple sky and the fairy lights coming into their own, Harry materialised at Emily's side.

'Dance with me,' he said. 'I haven't had a moment alone with you all evening, not even time to tell you that you look absolutely stunning in that red thing.' His eyes, very bright, searched her face. Had she bought it for him? Or was it a kind of defiant statement, telling the world that she wasn't afraid to look sexy if she chose?

Emily wrinkled her nose in simulated disgust. That figure-hugging, miniskirted, satin 'red thing' had been an expensive impulse buy for the occasion, especially, if she was honest, for Harry. She had deliberately set out to buy something eye-catching and she had a feeling that he would wholeheartedly approve of her being impulsive for once. It had been a long time since she had dressed to please anybody but herself.

Not since— She slammed the memory of Mark away. He was of no consequence any more. He certainly wouldn't have approved of the dress, he was much too conservative. He would have considered it too daring with its halter collar, lowish cut neckline and V-cut back.

'You look pretty stunning yourself,' she said, admiring the snug-fitting black cord pants and black silk, open-necked shirt.

'Outfit bought specially to please you,' he said.

Had he? 'Well, it does,' she murmured, with a smile.

A few other couples were dancing on the wide, smooth patio. The music was slow and romantic, straight out of an old film—not surprising as he was an aficionado of old films.

His hand, warm on the small of her back, sent out tentacles of electricity as he steered her towards the patio. Gently he pulled her into his arms.

'I'm not very good at this sort of dancing,' she murmured. 'I haven't danced for ages.'

The slimy toad again. 'Let me guess. Mark didn't approve.'

'Something like that.'

'To hell with Mark. Just relax and go with me.'

She relaxed and found herself going with him, gliding effortlessly over the tiles.

'Know this tune?' he asked.

Emily shook her head.

'"That old black magic has me in its spell,"' he crooned melodiously, bending his head close to hers. '"That old black magic that you weave so well."'

'How lovely.'

'Lovely and true, Em. You're a witch and you weave your black magic around me, have done since the day we met—fatal.' He spoke lightly, but his eyes were dark and intense. He whirled her up to the end of the long patio, away from the lights shining out from the sitting room to where they were lit only by the fairy lights.

She hoped he couldn't see her cheeks flame to match her dress. She essayed a little laugh. 'How many glasses of wine have you had, Harry?'

'Believe me, it isn't the wine talking, love, it's just the plain, unvarnished truth.'

The dress had been a mistake. It had made him think… What the hell had she been trying to do—to him, to herself? It wasn't fair to him and it wasn't good for her. The way he was looking at her! That dull, gut-deep pain was back and her breasts felt full, as if they might burst out of the barely restraining material.

She pleated her brow in a frown. 'Harry, I'm sorry if I've given out the wrong signals. I—well, you know how I feel. Nothing's changed. I just wanted to be different tonight, that's why I bought this dress, but I didn't mean to—'

'To tease, drive me wild with desire, bewitch me?' He gave a throaty chuckle.

She was relieved to hear the chuckle. 'No, I didn't.'

'My dear Em, you do that whether you're dressed to kill or wearing a bloodied apron when you're working. That's what I meant by bewitched. It's you, dear girl, not the clothes you wear. And I certainly don't think that you've suddenly become a *femme fatale*. I don't intend to ravish you till you are ready—promise.'

He made it sound casual, joky, but she knew it was true. He was reassuring her. In the dim light she could just make out his quirky grin and raised eyebrows.

'Oh, Harry, I don't deserve a friend like you.' She

stretched up and kissed him hard on the mouth. He felt slightly bristly and smelt of his smoky cologne.

He said softly, 'Thanks for that. Now, let's carry on dancing. We are supposed to be hosting this do—mustn't neglect our guests.' And he whirled her back along the patio.

People began to drift off soon after midnight. Jane Porter and her husband, Jeff, were the first to go.

'I don't want to go. It's been a lovely party, but I'm dead on my feet,' said Jane, kissing Emily and Harry goodnight. 'Had a busy day. Missed you two and I'm on earlies tomorrow.' She pulled Emily aside while the men were talking and muttered, 'Don't tell me you're just good friends after all that smoochy dancing you did. Hurry up and make an honest man of him. You make a super team—you deserve each other.'

Emily produced a laugh. 'Well, I know you don't believe me, but we *are* just good friends.'

'You're dead right. I don't believe you. I don't know what game you're playing, but you're head over heels in love with each other.'

Head over heels in love. Was it that obvious to everyone, wondered Emily when she at last crawled into bed, or only to Jane who knew them both well? Not that it made any difference. There was nothing they could do about it...not while Tim... Perhaps when he went away to university... Her eyelids drooped. She tried to keep them open, to think...

CHAPTER TEN

THREE days later the fine weather came to an abrupt end as August was ushered in with an almighty thunderstorm. The weather, thought Emily, standing on the doorstep and wondering if the rain was going to ease up, matches how I feel—restless, stirred up, feeling that something should or was going to happen, though I don't know what.

She had felt this way ever since the party, swinging between high and low, sometimes happy, sometimes sad—an uncomfortable state of affairs that she didn't understand. To make matters worse, she had seen nothing of Harry since the party.

He had unexpectedly extended the weekend to include Monday and Tuesday, but was due back this morning. The first Emily had known of it was when she'd come downstairs on Sunday morning and found a note on the mat, addressed to her in Harry's large, firm scrawl.

Em, Didn't want to disturb you by phoning. Have to go to Bristol. Have arranged with Guy to cover. Will you water garden please? Harry.

She read the note several times. It didn't change. It was curt and to the point, as if he'd written it in a hurry—perhaps he'd had a phone call from his parents. He hadn't said why he had to go Bristol so suddenly and he certainly hadn't hinted at it on Saturday night so presumably he hadn't known then.

For that matter, they hadn't spoken much at all once

the guests had gone and only Mrs Stubbs remained to help with the clearing up—just chit-chat about how well the party had gone. But, then, they'd been tired so it wasn't surprising.

When they had almost finished, Harry had urged her to go to bed and Mrs Stubbs, who had been like a mother hen to her ever since she had helped nurse her through flu, had added her voice to his.

'Go on,' she'd said. 'You've been working flat out over this last week or so, what with the hospital and everything. We can finish off here.'

Emily had given in and taken herself off to her own cottage to bed and to sleep. Tired, she'd barely noticed that Harry hadn't given her his customary kiss, but had simply given her a quick hug, wished her goodnight and told her to sleep well... But she remembered it when she read the note the next morning.

Not that it was significant. It certainly had nothing to do with him taking himself off to Bristol, but it niggled. Whatever the reason for that, perhaps it was just as well after the hype of the party that they should have a cooling-off period to get back on their regular footing. Perhaps, she thought laconically.

The rain wasn't going to stop so she made a dash for the garage and with wet, cold fingers scrabbled to unlock the doors as uncertainly as her thoughts continued to scrabble around in her head.

It had been a lonely few days. Tim hadn't been around either. He'd spent all his time with Neil, working on some project that had required the use of the highly sophisticated computer belonging to Neil's father. Apparently, their own PCs hadn't been up to the job. And when they hadn't been locked onto a computer they'd been on the river, practising sculling with the youth club.

Well, that was something to cheer about, Emily reminded herself as, having got the doors unlocked, she struggled to pull them open. The fact that Tim could now put his foot flat to the ground and Bob Keefe had declared his muscles strong enough to take the strain of the foot and leg work involved in sculling was tremendous news.

Also, he was having longer sessions with Harry, kicking a ball around. Tim was over the moon. As he saw it, it was a halfway house to him achieving his goal of a place in the school's reserve team.

Winning the battle with the stuck doors, she dragged them open. In fact, there was much to celebrate so why wasn't she feeling on top of the world? Tim was doing fine. She would see Harry at work today so why, in spite of the butterflies of pleased anticipation fluttering in her stomach, did she have this vague feeling of uneasiness? Because of the cryptic note? Because he hadn't kissed her after the party? Because he hadn't phoned and the three days that he'd been away had dragged?

Dragged! Understatement, she thought wryly as, dripping wet, she let herself into her little yellow Beetle. His absence had been a long, drawn-out pain, something that had to be endured. Because it couldn't be cured?

She gritted her teeth. Now was not the time to dwell on it. She had to get to work. She turned the ignition key—nothing. Dead silence, not even a shudder. She tried again—not a flicker. The engine was as dead as a doornail. 'Damn!' She thumped the steering-wheel. 'Now what—a taxi?'

No, by the time it arrived she would be late for work. Harry would take her, even if she had to get a bus home if he was staying late. He must have come back last night, though she hadn't heard him because of the storm, and she was pretty sure he hadn't yet left. Perhaps he was going in late.

He was driving out of his garage as she rushed out of hers.

'Harry,' she shrieked. The wind and rain tore her voice away. She dashed across her gravelled drive, round the fence and slithered along his patio, waving to attract his attention, afraid that he might not see her. He didn't have to get out of the car to open and close the up-and-over door, just waved an electronic device at it.

He was doing that when he saw her, and leaned over to open the passenger door.

'Thanks,' she said breathlessly as she climbed in. Oh, it was good to see him. Her spine tingled.

Harry nodded. The garage door obeyed his remote and he closed the window against the pelting rain and turned to look at her, smiling slightly.

'Let me guess. Car won't start.'

'Right first time.'

She'd hoped for one of his lovely smiles and perhaps a welcoming hug, but nothing happened. He started the engine and stared ahead of him as they bowled down the drive. His profile looked stern, his mouth set, his hands white-knuckled on the steering-wheel. Something was wrong...something to do with his parents? Should she ask him how things had gone in Bristol?

Emily opened her mouth to speak, just as he said in a dry sort of voice, 'You know, it's time you gave that thing a decent burial. It's way past its sell-by date.'

He'd often teased her about her elderly Beetle, but not like this—polite and distant, as if he were just making conversation with a near stranger. But she wasn't a stranger, but a loving friend.

No, more than a friend. Harry is in love with me, and I...? But the vibes are all wrong, there's no connection

between us. She shivered. Why? What had happened to
make him so distant?

She gave herself a mental shake. Wondering about it
wasn't going to help or make it hurt less—she would
have to ask. She swallowed an enormous lump in her
throat and said softly, 'What's wrong, Harry? What sent
you haring off to Bristol at short notice? Are your parents ill?'

'No, they're fine—tough as they come.' He gave a
little quirky, affectionate smile. He loves them as Tim
and I loved Mum, she thought, but his voice was almost
cold as he said, 'I went to talk to them about an invitation to do a six-week work and lecture tour in the
States—perhaps longer.'

Six weeks or longer! He was going to be away for at
least *six weeks* and he hadn't said a word to her. Her
heart thudded down to somewhere deep in her stomach.
She licked suddenly dry lips.

'Why didn't you tell me?' she whispered.

'Because I didn't know how you'd react.'

'I don't know what you mean. How long have you
known?'

'Only since Saturday morning. I didn't want to say
anything before the party. In fact...'

'In fact?'

'I wanted to discuss it with you, but that rather de-
pended on what happened at the party. In the event, I
didn't think you'd care whether I was here or in
America.'

She looked at him in amazement. How could he think
such a thing? 'I don't understand. Of course I'd care—
care very much.'

'Would you, Em?' His voice was rough. 'God help
me, woman, I practically grovelled at your feet, offered
marriage again on Saturday night. I'm not made of stone,

I'm a full-blooded, sexual man with all a man's normal appetites. I'm getting tired of waiting and hoping without any encouragement. It's hard to see a future for us—that's why I discussed the offer with my parents rather than with you.'

Appetites, sexual appetites! She felt both sad and angry. It always came down to that in the end. The pain stirred in her guts again. Hell, she had appetites too. She couldn't pretend any more. She loved Harry, as much as he said he loved her. She longed to make love to him, wanted to marry him, but—it was a huge but—she had Tim to think about. She wouldn't hurt him, not even to be with Harry.

He'd been so patient, but now he'd all but issued an ultimatum. Either she married him or...a bleak future empty of even his friendship? And if he went to the States for a short tour, he might be head-hunted, asked to take up a permanent post. Wasn't that what happened to many of our top surgeons?

They turned into the hospital complex.

Harry parked in the consultants' area. He undid his seat belt and leaned across and undid hers. She shrank back in her seat. His lips curled into a bitter, lopsided smile.

He said in a dry voice, 'It's all right, Em, I'm not going to touch you. We'll finish this discussion tonight, see if we can resolve anything. I've got an admin meeting so I won't be home till about half eight. If he's around, tell Tim we want to talk and don't want to be interrupted.'

'But—'

'No buts. If you don't, I will. He'll understand. Try treating him like a responsible adult for once, Emily, slip the apron-strings. He's got two good feet to stand on now.'

'How—how dare you?' she spluttered.

'I dare because I love you both,' he said quietly. 'By the way, how are you getting home?'

Her immediate reaction was to say that it was none of his business but that was childish, and what he had just said about loving them made it impossible. Supposing he took her at her word…ended everything… The thought made her blood run like ice in her veins.

Through teeth clenched to stop them chattering, she said, 'Bus.'

'Take a taxi.' He took a note out of his wallet. 'My treat.'

It was pointless to refuse, he would only insist.

'Thank you.'

She got through the day on autopilot: cleaning dirty wounds; staunching blood; holding vomit bowls under chins, being endlessly reassuring. Stitching, bandaging, cuddling crying babies, giving anti-tetanus jabs, pain-killing jabs—the chores were neverending. Patients in pain, patients hysterical, in one case a patient dying and grieving relatives to be comforted. She dealt with everything with her usual quiet efficiency and warm sympathy.

Of Harry she saw little, except when he assisted with the abortive attempt to resuscitate the woman who had subsequently died. The team, as always, had worked flat out to save the badly injured woman, but eventually he had, with everyone's agreement, called a halt. His eyes, sad and compassionate, had met hers briefly over the dead body before he turned away to throw his soiled apron and gloves into the bin.

For the rest of the day she continued to converse, smile and even joke, and nobody guessed that she was numb inside, zombielike, her heart a lead weight in her chest. Even her mind was numb, empty, permanently fixed on hold. It was as if nature for the moment had anaesthetised her so that she couldn't think.

Eventually, the long, exhausting day came to an end, and at six o'clock she dragged herself out to the waiting taxi.

Harry watched her leave from his office window. He could see how exhausted she was and empathised with her, but he didn't feel much better himself. It was emotional rather than physical exhaustion. Their conversation on the way to work had left them both drained, and he was mentally preparing himself for tonight's meeting.

Perhaps he'd been too hard on her, perhaps he should give her more time? Perhaps they should go on just as good friends for the time being, which was what she had pleaded for? She'd had a hell of a nine months. But could he cope with things as they were for much longer? He loved her with a depth and passion that was frightening, but he also lusted after her in the good old-fashioned sense of the word. His body told him that whenever he was near her or thought about her, which was practically constantly.

He still wasn't sure how much of the trauma she'd suffered had been due to her mother's death, Tim's disablement or her fiancé's desertion. Or how much stemmed from further back and her father's brutal treatment of her mother, especially where her fears of a close relationship were concerned. Surely he had been right to force the issue, insist on them talking it through.

Then all he had to do, he thought wryly, was get her to trust him, convince her that love and trust go together—the basis, as he'd been reminded this weekend when he'd visited his parents, of a happy marriage.

Winning her trust was as vital as winning her love—that was the bottom line.

The admin meeting wound up a bit early and he was home by eight o'clock.

It was hot and humid. The rain had long since stopped, but it was still overcast and there was still thunder about. He had time to shower and change and give Tim the opportunity to disappear before he showed himself next door. That was if Emily hadn't chickened out of passing on the message that they wanted their own space. Of course, they could have met at his cottage but somehow he had the feeling that she would be more relaxed on home territory, and it had also given him the chance to say what he had about easing off on Tim. They both needed to let go a bit.

He saw the strange car parked in front of their cottage as he walked along the patio. His heart sank. Damn, a visitor, tonight of all nights. He prayed whoever it was would soon depart.

About to unlock his front door, he heard the sound of raised voices floating out of the open windows next door.

No, not voices—a single voice, male, aggressive, angry!

Holding his breath, Harry stood stock-still and unashamedly listened, trying to make out what was being said. His skin prickled and the hair on the back of his neck stood up. A man shouting at Emily, Tim? What should he do about it? Was it someone they knew or a stranger? Would it embarrass Emily if he made his presence known?

The voice was raised to a threatening shout. Harry heard the words 'If you don't, I'll…' Then Emily and Tim's voices came as an indistinct murmur.

He waited no longer. If he was interfering—tough. They were being threatened. He pushed his way round the fence, and instinctively ducked under the window-sill as he tried to walk soundlessly across the gravel. The porch door was ajar. He slipped into the small hall. The door to the sitting room was open.

He took in the tableau before him. A tall, broad-shouldered man stood with his back to him, swaying slightly, with one hand raised shakily in a half-hearted threatening gesture. Drunk? Emily and Tim were facing him, looking both defiant and scared.

It was obvious that they knew the man...and so did he! There was no mistaking his back view—a taller, larger version of Tim's, and the thick black hair, the shape of the head, Tim's head.

Their father! It had to be. The man who had terrified them as children, the man who had beaten up his wife. A man with a temper.

Silently, Harry stepped into the room and stood behind him.

'Good evening,' he said, in a deep, drawling voice.

Emily and Tim flicked their eyes away from the interloper and stared at him, wide-eyed. The man whirled and uttered an obscenity.

Harry said mildly, 'Sorry to butt in, but I heard raised voices. It sounded a bit rough and I wondered if you two were all right.' He looked directly at Emily and Tim.

They nodded speechlessly. Expressions of relief flitted across their faces.

'And who the hell are you?' the visitor snarled, his speech slightly slurred, his hands up as if about to throw a punch. His bloodshot eyes blazed angrily as they tried to focus on Harry.

'A close friend, a neighbour, and you are...?' Harry replied. The question hung in the air. He kept his voice pleasant and even, but his face was grim and unsmiling and Emily saw his hands ball into white-knuckled fists at his side.

She was suddenly galvanised into action. She stepped forward and made a placatory little gesture and said in a firm voice, 'Harry, this is my father, Geoffrey Prince. Dad, this is Harry Paradine, head of the casualty department where I work and, as he said, also our friend and our next-door neighbour.' She looked at each of them in turn, her eyes pleading with them to keep their cool.

Slowly Harry unclenched his fists, knowing that, except in defence of Emily and Tim, it was unlikely that he would ever have used them. It had been an automatic response to their father's aggressive pose. But it wasn't his style. Emily was right—they must try to be civilised about this.

He gave her a quick, reassuring smile and, for her sake, held out his hand to her father. 'Mr Prince...'

Geoffrey Prince ignored it. He squared his shoulders, stretching the expensive cloth of his well-cut business suit in an obvious attempt to pull himself together. Had he not been drunk he would have looked distinguished. He said with heavy sarcasm, 'Well, Mr...er...Paradine, as you so elegantly put it, you have butted into a private conversation so you can butt out again—you're not wanted here.'

'Yes, he is,' said Emily and Tim in unison.

Tim moved swiftly across the room and stood next to Harry. He touched Harry's arm. 'Please stay.' His voice was suddenly gruff and uncertain.

Harry put an arm round his shoulders. 'Of course, if you and Emily want me to...' He looked at Emily.

She nodded. 'We'd value your advice, Harry, as an impartial observer.'

'No, we bloody wouldn't,' shouted Geoffrey Prince. 'You keep out of this.' He lunged at Harry, tripped and would have fallen if Harry hadn't caught him.

Harry lowered him into an armchair. The older man closed his eyes and slumped like a rag doll, his head lolling on his chest.

He was very drunk.

Harry said harshly, 'We'll leave him for a few minutes, then fill him up with strong black coffee.'

'I'll make it,' volunteered Tim, clearly glad to get out of the room.

Emily stood for a moment, surveying her father, then walked over to the window. Harry joined her. Together they stood side by side, gazing across the gardens bathed in evening sunlight.

Harry longed to take her into his arms and comfort her, but he guessed she wasn't ready for any demonstration of affection. She was stiff with embarrassment on her father's behalf.

As if to a stranger, she said distantly, 'Thank you, you've been very kind.'

He replied briskly, 'Not at all, my pleasure. By the way, your father's not going to be fit to drive anywhere. Is he staying in the area or planning to return to London or wherever?'

'He's booked in at the Grand in Chellminster. He said he was staying there till we'd finished our business… But, Harry, I don't want to see him again.' Her voice was suddenly brittle, hard. 'Do you know, he didn't even come to Mother's funeral, or communicate, and now he wants part of the money she left.'

'But surely all that was tied up when they got divorced?'

'It was, but he thought he could frighten us into giving him something more—he always was a bully and greedy. But he's not getting a penny—what's left is for Tim's education.'

Her neat, rounded chin tilted defiantly, her shining black bob of hair swung back from her face and her brilliant blue eyes sparkled with anger and determination. Harry had never loved her so much. Again he wanted to take her in his arms and again resisted the temptation. She was confiding in him, trusting him, and that's what mattered.

He took her hand and squeezed it. 'You won't have to talk to him again,' he said, his voice firm. 'Any future communications will be conducted through solicitors though, as I see it, he hasn't got a hope in hell of changing the terms of the will. I'll make sure he understands that when I run him back to his hotel.'

Emily looked startled. 'Oh, Harry, you don't have to do that. I can order a taxi. You've done enough. If you hadn't come when you did I think he might have got really rough, like he did sometimes when we were children.' She gave him a tight little smile. 'Funny, isn't it? He always looked such a gentleman that no one guessed it was just a veneer—what he was like to live with.' Her eyes filled with sudden tears, which she blinked back furiously.

Harry looked down at her, his eyes full of love. He raised her hand to his lips and brushed his lips across her fingers. 'Elegant clothes,' he said softly, 'do not necessarily make a gentleman, which is why I'm going to drive him back in his car and not give him any excuse for returning to threaten you again, my dearest love.'

Hours later Emily sat up, punched her pillow, turned it over and lay down again with her hot cheek pressed to the cool side.

My dearest love. He'd whispered the words with great

tenderness, and they continued to revolve in her head, together with all the other tumultuous thoughts of the eventful evening.

She had come close then to throwing herself into Harry's arms and declaring her love for him, but Tim had arrived with the coffee and the moment had passed.

Nearly an hour had flown past as they'd poured gallons of coffee down her father's throat and walked him around until he'd been sober enough to agree to Harry driving him to his hotel.

Arguing and reluctant, he had handed over the keys. 'But I'll be back,' he'd said truculently as she and Harry had bundled him into the car.

'Over my dead body,' muttered Harry as he took his place in the driving seat. He leaned out of the window and smiled reassuringly at Emily and Tim. 'Don't worry,' he promised, 'it's going to be all right. He'll never bother you again—I'll make sure of that.'

'Wow, do you think they'll have a punch-up?' asked Tim in a rather awed voice, edged with excitement, as the car sped away down the drive.

He half hopes they will, thought Emily. He's young enough to believe that a fist fight will solve the problem. Then she remembered Harry's clenched fists earlier in the evening when he had faced her father. But that had been an instinctive gesture, more in defence of her and Tim than a desire to be aggressive. He was a caring doctor, dedicated to healing wounds not causing them.

She gave her brother a wry smile. 'No,' she said confidently, 'Harry won't resort to a punch-up. He's much too intelligent and civilised for that. I don't know what he'll say, but he'll just talk to Dad and convince him that he has nothing to gain by coming back.'

Tim nodded. 'Yeah, I think you're right. If anyone

can do it, Harry can. He's brilliant—he sort of makes you feel safe.'

Emily felt a warm glow in the pit of her stomach. 'Yes, he does, doesn't he?' she said softly.

The warm glow was still with her when she woke the next morning and pulsated into a sunburst when the phone rang...Harry! It had to be him.

There was a hint of laughter in his deep voice as he murmured in her ear, 'Presuming your little Beetle hasn't done a Lazarus and risen from the dead, I'll give you a lift into work in my trusty steed.'

She chuckled and said rather breathlessly, 'My knight in shining armour to the rescue...again.'

There was a different note in his voice as he said softly, 'At your service, Em...always. See you at seven sharp.'

The phone clicked.

At your service always. And he meant it. Her heart rocketed against her ribs. 'And I didn't even thank him for last night,' she muttered *sotto voce*.

She tried to do so half an hour later when they were bowling along toward Chellminster.

'About last night,' she began, 'I can't tell you how much—'

'Don't say anything. There's no need, my darling.' He covered her clenched hands with one large one. 'It's over and done with. I did what I had to do, wanted to do. I'm just so sorry that it ever happened. But it won't happen again. Trust me, you have my word on it.'

Trust him. Emily blinked back tears. 'Oh, Harry, I've been such a fool.' Her voice wobbled.

Harry took his hand from hers while he negotiated a roundabout and moved into a line of traffic. Before he could replace it they were turning into the hospital entrance. His bleeper went as they parked in the consultants' area.

He leaned across and kissed her swiftly, sweetly, on the mouth. 'We'll talk tonight. I'll be home about seven,' he said.

Like yesterday, A and E was busy, and Emily saw hardly anything of Harry, but there the similarity ended. Gone were the blues of the previous day—the numbness, the sense of foreboding. She was quietly euphoric. The same succession of injured and battered bodies passed through the department, and she dealt with them with the same warmth and sympathy, but today she didn't have to call on years of practice to do her job. It was effortless.

Today's world was full of hope. Suddenly all her problems seemed solvable...though how, she wasn't sure.

She went off duty at five. It was warm and the sun was shining so she caught the bus home—no need for a taxi today.

The cottage was empty when she got back. Blessedly detached, feeling as if she were floating on air, she showered and changed into a comfortable but flattering sundress of soft blue cotton. She was standing outside the porch, combing her damp hair into its neat bob, when Tim jogged up the drive. He was grinning from ear to ear and looking incredibly happy. His eyes, as blue as hers, were sparkling as he came to a halt in front of her.

Emily tilted her head to smile at him. He was getting taller every day. 'You look like the Cheshire cat in *Alice*,' she said. 'Very pleased with yourself.'

He took a deep breath and stood with his feet apart, his hands resting on his narrow hips. He said, 'I've been to see Mr Coomes, our sports master.'

'What—at his house when he's on holiday? Poor man.'

'He didn't mind. He's been asking me for weeks how I was getting on. He'd noticed that I was walking much better. I just had to tell him that Bob thinks I'm fit enough to play football again. We had a knockabout in his garden—and guess what?'

She looked at his radiant face. 'Tell me.'

'He's going to give me a trial run directly we get back to school! I said I'd make it, Em, didn't I?'

'You did. Oh, Tim, it's marvellous, I'm so happy for you.' She wanted to hug him but, instead, gave him a punch on the shoulder. 'Harry will be too.'

Tim's face was suddenly serious, softened, and he looked older. 'It wouldn't have happened if it hadn't been for Harry. He made me stick at it,' he said. 'He's a very special sort of guy.'

'Yes, he is very special,' Emily said softly.

Tim was watching her intently. 'Do you like him a lot, Em? Are you keen on him?'

She stared at him and felt the colour ebb and flow in her cheeks.

'Well, are you keen on Harry?' He sounded impatient.

Her breath caught in her throat. She tried to think of something innocuous to say but couldn't. Bereft of words, she nodded.

He looked triumphant. 'Thought so. Thought you fancied each other. So why don't you two get together—get married or something? It'd be brilliant. We'd be like a real family, like we were before Mum died. Give it a thought, Em.' He looked at his watch and made for the door. 'Must get changed—rowing practice.'

For a long time after he'd gone Emily sat on the sun lounger to 'give it a thought'. She was shattered. That Tim had noticed so much shook her to the core. She'd thought he was like any teenager, absorbed in his own affairs, not noticing what went on around him, but he'd noticed that she and Harry...fancied each other. And he wanted them to be married, be a 'real' family.

She blew her nose hard and swallowed the lump lodged in her throat. Of course, it wasn't surprising that he felt like that. It made sense. Harry was his role model, the ideal father figure that he'd never had.

As if a veil were lifting, it slowly dawned on her that there was no reason why she shouldn't marry Harry now. Tim wouldn't be hurt. He wanted—*needed*—Harry as a brother-in-law... Suddenly it was crystal clear. She had been using Tim as a shield, telling herself he would be hurt if she gave into her love for Harry, when all the time she had been afraid for herself. Afraid Harry would hurt her, as Mark had hurt her?

Impossible!

She closed her eyes in anguish. How could she have thought such a thing? He had proved over the months that his love was deep and unshakeable. And she loved him—there were no doubts left.

No doubts left! She gave a huge sigh of pure happiness. She could tell Harry that the waiting game was over.

CHAPTER ELEVEN

THE evening was blue and gold, and warm and loud with the buzzing of bees. Her feet hardly touching the ground as she savoured the scent of honeysuckle, roses and cinnamon pinks, Emily walked slowly up Harry's garden path. She had taken the long way round to give herself time to collect her thoughts and prepare what she was going to say to Harry, although she had already rehearsed it several times.

She reached the top of the path and floated up the steps to the patio. He was waiting for her, filling the doorway of his cottage with his tall, solid frame—rugged and reassuring in lightweight denims and a crisp white shirt, unbuttoned at the neck to reveal the cluster of coppery curls at his throat.

Emily stood still for a moment, drinking in the sheer, pulsing masculinity that emanated from him. She could almost feel the warmth radiate from him, reaching out to her. A thrill of delight, slightly tinged with apprehension, rippled through her as she drew nearer. She caught her breath. She knew what she had to say, but not quite how to say it.

Then Harry smiled his wide tender smile and her apprehension melted away. His dark eyes, eloquent, full of love, crinkled at the corners, making her bones turn to water. Without a word he opened his arms wide, and Emily went into them.

'Oh, Harry,' she murmured, as he crushed her against his chest and nuzzled the top of her head. 'What a fool I've been. I've given you such a hard time.'

Keeping his arms round her, Harry steered her into the sitting room, sat on the sofa and pulled her onto his lap. 'You reckon?' he said, his eyes gently amused, twinkling. He smoothed her hair back from her face and kissed her on her forehead. 'Want to tell me about it, dearest heart?'

Dearest heart! She would never tire of hearing him say that in his deep, honeyed voice. Her heart somersaulted, then righted itself.

'Yes,' she whispered.

Haltingly at first, and then more fluently, she recounted the conversation she'd had with Tim and the illuminating thoughts that had followed.

'So you see—' her voice was a little tremulous '—suddenly everything became plain. I realised that I had been hiding behind Tim, pretending that even if I loved you I couldn't marry you for fear of hurting him. But it wasn't true, Harry. It was because I was scared and bitter and afraid that *I* might be hurt again. I just couldn't risk it.'

Harry took her face in his hands, cupping her chin and smoothing his thumbs across her trembling lips. 'And could you risk it now, Em? Do you love me enough, trust me enough, to marry me, let me care for you, cherish you?'

Unflinching, her eyes met his. 'Yes,' she said firmly, 'I do.' She slid her hands round his neck, tangled her fingers in his hair and pulled his head closer. Gently she rubbed the tip of her nose to his. 'Make love to me, Harry,' she murmured against his mouth.

'Is this a reward for patience?' he murmured back.

'No, it's because I *want* you, *need* you, and I want to show you how much I love you.'

She could see little gold flecks in his dark brown eyes

as they smiled into hers. 'That sounds like reason enough,' he said evenly.

'You ain't seen nothing yet,' she said huskily, on a chuckle of laughter.

He gathered her tighter into his arms and stood up in one fluid movement. She could feel the ripple of the muscles in his arms and chest, hear the steady beating of his heart, feel the silky yet crisply curling hairs against her cheek.

'Are you issuing a challenge—my prowess against yours?' he asked, carrying her through the hall, up the stairs and through a door into his bedroom—like hers, with sloping ceilings, she noticed as he crossed the room, but larger. With elaborate care he laid her on the wide double bed, bathed in slanting evening sunlight shining through the lattice windows, and stood, looking down at her.

'A challenge? Could be,' she breathed, her whole body pulsing with longing, overwhelmed with the desire to kiss and caress him, arouse him till their naked bodies melted into each other. 'Try me.'

He took in a deep breath which stretched his shirt across his broad chest. She could see a pulse throbbing in his throat.

His eyes darkened until they were almost black. 'Oh, I will,' he said in a deep, throaty voice. Then, arching an eyebrow, he added, 'I don't suppose, my love, that you are on the Pill—are you?'

Her cheeks flamed and her hand flew to her mouth. 'Lord, I didn't think of that.'

He grinned and bent over and brushed his lips across her cheek. 'Then you'll have to excuse me for one moment.'

She waited, pulses racing, breath coming unevenly,

loins aching, sweating a little, longing to feel his body heavy on hers.

A couple of minutes later he returned, wearing a short, white towelling robe, loosely belted. He knelt on the bed beside her, crouched and stroked an errant hair back from her face. 'You're sure about this, Em, my darling, aren't you?'

She heaved a sigh and her blue eyes sparkled between her long lashes. 'I've never been more sure of anything in my life,' she purred, offering him her pouting mouth.

Harry's closed over it in a long, lingering kiss. He undressed her slowly. His love-making was exquisite. Slow, passionate yet gentle, as his large, capable hands moved about her body and his lips and tongue delicately discovered every vulnerable curve and crevice. His tongue darted and explored. He licked and kissed and nuzzled over and over again, bringing her almost to the peak of fulfilment, and then held back until at last, in one glorious moment, they reached the ultimate peak together.

Breathless, whispering endearments, they remained wrapped in each other's arms until the golden sun set, the room turned to crimson and dusk fell.

'Tim will be back soon,' murmured Emily, nuzzling Harry's nose, pressing her bruised lips to his and wincing as his bearded chin rasped against her smooth cheek.

Harry kissed her eyelids, nose and mouth, then unwrapped his arms and propped himself up on one elbow.

'Have I told you lately that I love you?' he asked.

'Not for all of five seconds.'

'Then I must remedy that,' he said softly. 'I love you, Emily Prince, because you are kind and loving and caring, and a warm and passionate woman—a complete package.'

Emily, too, propped herself up on her elbow so that

she could face him. She said in the low, husky voice that he loved, '*You've* made me complete, Harry. Thank you, my darling, for being so patient, bearing with me all this time when I tried to freeze you out. I'm so sorry. I'll make it up to you—'

He put his fingers across her mouth. 'Shh—no regrets. You put me on my mettle, forced me to play knight to my fair lady—man the hunter and all that.'

'Did you ever think of giving up?'

'Not really, though I came near it on the night of the party. That's why I went to Bristol—to talk to my parents about you as well as the American offer.'

'They must have thought you mad to want to marry me—a cold, detached, ungrateful female who had rejected your love.'

'No, they didn't see you like that. They saw you as a warm, loving woman who'd had a rotten deal from life and cheerfully given up a hell of a lot to care for her kid brother. They also saw you as the only woman I had ever loved, and thought me mad to consider backing down, but they did think a little space between us might be a good idea for a short while.'

A slight smile lifted the corners of her mouth. 'And what do you think, Harry?' she asked huskily.

He shook his head. 'No longer a good idea. I couldn't bear to be parted from you, not even for six weeks. I think that we should mix business with pleasure and honeymoon in the good old US of A, with perhaps a side trip to the Caribbean before we come home. How does that sound to you, dearest heart?' He leaned forward and kissed her with infinite gentleness on her swollen lips.

'I think it's the perfect solution,' Emily said softly, her eyes shining with naked love, 'but before the

honeymoon comes the wedding, my darling. We have
waited long enough. Please let us be married soon.'

Harry stroked her cheek. 'I think,' he murmured, 'that
might be arranged.'

Three weeks later, escorted by Tim, walking tall and
straight, Emily floated down the aisle of the hospital
chapel to join Harry, waiting for her at the altar. She felt
his large reassuring hand clasp hers and squeeze it
gently.

The chaplain began the service. 'We are gathered here
together...'

MILLS & BOON®

Medical Romance™

COMING NEXT MONTH

VALENTINE MAGIC by Margaret Barker

Dr Tim Fielding found it impossible to believe that Katie didn't want a relationship, but she was determined to remain independent and *definitely* single!

THE FAMILY TOUCH by Sheila Danton

The attraction between Callum Smith and Fran Bergmont was potent, but as a very new single mother, she needed time before risking involvement again.

THE BABY AFFAIR by Marion Lennox

Jock Blaxton adored every baby he delivered, so why didn't he have his own? Having his baby wasn't a problem for Tina Rafter, but Jock?

A COUNTRY CALLING by Leah Martyn

A&E wasn't easy, and dealing with Nick Cavallo was no picnic either for Melanie Stewart, so it surprised her when they became friends—and more?

Available from 5th February 1999

Available at most branches of WH Smith, Tesco, Asda, Martins, Borders, Easons, Volume One/James Thin and most good paperback bookshops

ELIZABETH GAGE

When Dusty brings home her young fiancé, he
is everything her mother Rebecca Lowell could
wish for her daughter, *and for herself*...

The Lowell family's descent into darkness
begins with one bold act, one sin
committed in an otherwise blameless life.
This time there's no absolution in...

Confession

MIRA®   AVAILABLE FROM JANUARY 1999

He's a cop, she's his prime suspect

MARY LYNN BAXTER

HARD CANDY

He's crossed the line no cop ever should.
He's involved with a suspect—his
prime suspect.

Falling for the wrong man is far down her
list of troubles.

Until he arrests her for murder.

MIRA® Available from 18th December 1998

2 FREE

books and a surprise gift!

We would like to take this opportunity to thank you for reading this Mills & Boon® book by offering you the chance to take TWO more specially selected titles from the Medical Romance™ series absolutely FREE! We're also making this offer to introduce you to the benefits of the Reader Service™—

- ★ FREE home delivery
- ★ FREE gifts and competitions
- ★ FREE monthly Newsletter
- ★ Books available before they're in the shops
- ★ Exclusive Reader Service discounts

Accepting these FREE books and gift places you under no obligation to buy, you may cancel at any time, even after receiving your free shipment. Simply complete your details below and return the entire page to the address below. *You don't even need a stamp!*

YES! Please send me 2 free Medical Romance books and a surprise gift. I understand that unless you hear from me, I will receive 4 superb new titles every month for just £2.30 each, postage and packing free. I am under no obligation to purchase any books and may cancel my subscription at any time. The free books and gift will be mine to keep in any case.

M9EA

Ms/Mrs/Miss/Mr...............................Initials ....
BLOCK CAPITALS PLEASE

Surname ....

Address ....

....

....Postcode.....................................

Send this whole page to:
THE READER SERVICE, FREEPOST CN81, CROYDON, CR9 3WZ
(Eire readers please send coupon to: P.O. BOX 4546, DUBLIN 24.)

Offer not valid to current Reader Service subscribers to this series. We reserve the right to refuse an application and applicants must be aged 18 years or over. Only one application per household. Terms and prices subject to change without notice. Offer expires 31st July 1999. As a result of this application, you may receive further offers from Harlequin Mills & Boon and other carefully selected companies. If you would prefer not to share in this opportunity please write to The Data Manager at the address above.

Medical Romance is being used as a trademark.

JOANN ROSS

a woman's heart

In *A Woman's Heart*, JoAnn Ross has created a
rich, lyrical love story about land, community,
family and the very special bond between a man
who doesn't believe in anything and a woman
who believes in him.

MIRA®   **Available from February**